"I'm sorry

"About?" Adrian asked as he paused in his task of sorting through the box.

"Misjudging you."

He met her gaze, his expression unreadable. "Are you so sure yet that you did?"

She nodded. "Pretty sure."

After a moment of searching her face, he said, "Thank you for that, then." He stood and held out a hand. "I know you don't have all afternoon. Shall we move on?"

Lucy stared at his hand, absurdly afraid that if she laid hers in it, she truly would be sorry.

Because touching him might be dangerous to her peace of mind.

Dear Reader,

Like many of my books, the plot of *Someone Like Her* came to me from a newspaper article. I recall only the gist of it: an elderly homeless woman died in a small town, and community members who had cared for her all contributed to pay for her funeral. The notion intrigued me. The homeless tend to congregate in cities. Why did she choose not just a small town, but *that* small town? Did she really have no family? I imagined what family—a son, say—would think to learn that Mom had lived this kind of life, lost in one way, yet somehow having found a real home, too.

Partway through writing *Someone Like Her,* I realized that I was revisiting a theme that seems to captivate me. I write often about the people missing from the lives of my characters. I often think that never knowing the fate of someone you love would be worse than burying that person. In *Someone Like Her,* Adrian Rutledge has been haunted by his mother's disappearance from his life when he was a child. Now in a coma after having been hit by a car, his mother may never open her eyes and recognize him. Yet, guided by the kind restaurant owner who tracked him down, he has the chance to unravel the past by meeting his mother again, through the eyes of townsfolk who knew her. Perhaps Adrian *couldn't* love until he remembered who he was before he lost his mother. The miracle is that his mother has brought him to the woman he wants in his life forever.

This story moved me from the beginning. I hope you feel the same.

Best,

Janice Kay Johnson

P.S. If you want to write, please do so c/o Harlequin Books, 225 Duncan Mill Road, Don Mills, ON M3B 3K9, Canada.

SOMEONE LIKE HER
Janice Kay Johnson

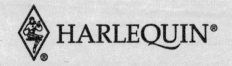

TORONTO • NEW YORK • LONDON
AMSTERDAM • PARIS • SYDNEY • HAMBURG
STOCKHOLM • ATHENS • TOKYO • MILAN • MADRID
PRAGUE • WARSAW • BUDAPEST • AUCKLAND

Recycling programs
for this product may
not exist in your area.

ISBN-13: 978-0-373-71558-9
ISBN-10:   0-373-71558-7

SOMEONE LIKE HER

www.eHarlequin.com

Printed in U.S.A.

ABOUT THE AUTHOR

The author of more than sixty books for children and adults, Janice Kay Johnson writes Harlequin Superromance novels about love and family—about the way generations connect, and the power our earliest experiences have on us throughout life. Her 2007 novel *Snowbound* won a RITA® Award from Romance Writers of America for Best Contemporary Series Romance. A former librarian, Janice raised two daughters in a small rural town north of Seattle, Washington. She loves to read, and is an active volunteer and board member for Purrfect Pals, a no-kill cat shelter.

Books by Janice Kay Johnson

HARLEQUIN SUPERROMANCE
1092—THE GIFT OF CHRISTMAS
    "Undercover Santa"
1140—TAKING A CHANCE†
1153—THE PERFECT MOM†
1166—THE NEW MAN†
1197—MOMMY SAID
    GOODBYE
1228—REVELATIONS
1273—WITH CHILD
1332—OPEN SECRET*
1351—LOST CAUSE*
1383—KIDS BY CHRISTMAS*
1405—FIRST COMES BABY
1454—SNOWBOUND
1489—THE MAN BEHIND
    THE COP

†Under One Roof
*Lost…But Not Forgotten

HARLEQUIN ANTHOLOGY
A MOTHER'S LOVE
    "Daughter of the Bride"

HARLEQUIN EVERLASTING LOVE
21—CHRISTMAS
    PRESENTS AND PAST

HARLEQUIN SINGLE TITLE
WRONG TURN
    "Missing Molly"

SIGNATURE SELECT SAGA
DEAD WRONG

CHAPTER ONE

"EVERY TABLE FULL except the reserved one, and it's a Tuesday." Carrying two glasses of iced tea, Mabel paused to grin at Lucy Peterson. "Those new soups are a hit."

She continued into the crowded dining room of the café. Lucy, who had just finished ringing up a customer, looked around with satisfaction. Mabel was right. Business kept getting better and better.

The bell over the door rang. Lucy's head turned as her guest slipped in, her carriage confident, her gaze shy. The hat lady.

Last time Lucy had seen her, the day before yesterday, she'd carried herself decorously and yet with regal authority. The pillbox hat had said it all. She was often Queen Elizabeth—the second, she always emphasized. She didn't actually look much like Queen Elizabeth II, being slender rather than matronly in build, with hair that had been blond when she first appeared in Middleton, perhaps ten years ago. Now her hair was primarily white, as wispy and flyaway as the woman whose head it crowned.

But today, she wore a flower-printed dress and a broad-brimmed hat festooned with flowers. Her face was softer, her carriage more youthful, her gaze vaguer.

This was always the awkward moment. Lucy had to pretend she knew who Middleton's one and only homeless person was. Calling her by the wrong name seemed so insulting.

Talk in the café hadn't dimmed at all. Everyone knew the hat lady was a project of Lucy's. Lucy's Aunt Marian called, "Your majesty," and resumed her one-sided conversation with Uncle Sidney, who almost never said a word, and failed entirely to notice the hat lady's astonished stare.

Lucy went to her and said in a gentle voice, "I'm so glad you could come to lunch today. Your table's right here, by the window. Did you see the crocus are blooming?"

The hat lady smiled at her, her face crinkling with pleasure. "God's gifts put man's best dreams to shame."

Okay. It was a clue. She still had a British accent, which was mostly a given, although not long ago she'd been Elizabeth Taylor, the accent wholly American. She had an astonishing gift for accents; a few months ago, she'd done a splendid Eliza Doolittle, starting with a nearly indecipherable Cockney accent skillfully revised over several weeks until she spoke with a pure, somewhat stilted upper-crust accent worthy of the most carefully tutored student.

Lucy had taken to rereading English literature and watching classic films so she wouldn't be completely lost every time the hat lady changed personas.

"Please. Sit down." Lucy gestured her to the tiny table for two in front of the bow window, which she'd reserved especially for the hat lady. Yellow and purple crocuses bloomed in the windowbox outside. Her shopping cart, neatly packed, was parked on the sidewalk where she could see it. That was why Lucy always saved the window seat for her. "Would you care for tea?"

"Please."

She gazed with seeming delight and no boredom out the window until Lucy returned with a teapot, loose tea steeping inside. One did not offer the hat lady tea improperly made.

From the menu she chose only soup and a scone. Lucy had tried persuading her to have a hearty meal when she was here, but had never succeeded.

"Won't you join me?" she did ask, with vague surprise as if unaware there was a busy restaurant around them, and that Lucy was in charge.

"I might sit down with you for a moment a little later," she promised. Her friend had aged noticeably these past few months, Lucy noted with dismay. Her spine was as straight as ever, her pinkie finger extended as she sipped tea, but she must have lost weight. She seemed frail today. If only she could be persuaded to settle into a rented room! Hiding her worry, Lucy asked, "How are you?"

She tilted her face up. Her blue eyes, fading like her hair, seemed unusually perceptive all of a sudden, as if she saw the doubts and unhappiness Lucy scarcely acknowledged even to herself. In a voice too low for anyone at neighboring tables to hear, she said, "I might ask you the same."

Lucy's mouth opened and closed.

After a moment, the cornflower-blue eyes softened, looked inward, and she murmured, "Did you know the sorrow comes with the years?"

"I…" Something seemed to clog Lucy's throat. "Yes. Yes, I did."

This smile seemed to forgive her. "Grief may be joy misunderstood."

Oh! That line she'd heard. Somewhere, sometime. It had to have been written, or said, by a Beth, or Liza, Lizbet, or Elizabeth… Yes! Lucy thought in triumph. Elizabeth Barrett Browning. Of course. The hat lady was very fond of her poetry. Only, the first couple of things she said had seemed so sensible, if also profound, Lucy hadn't recognized them as poetry.

"Miss Browning," she said, "I'm so glad you could join me today."

She meant to get back to the hat lady and sit with her, as promised. She did. But the kitchen ran out of spinach, and she had to race to Safeway for more, then Aunt Marian expressed her opinion at some length on the very peculiar soup—which was delicious, but she did miss the split pea Lucy used to offer. And then Samantha, Lucy's youngest and most compatible sister, who had recently opened a bed-and-breakfast inn, suggested they join together to put on a murder mystery weekend, with the guests staying at Doveport B and B and Lucy catering the meals. Samantha had scarcely left than Lucy's niece Bridget came in to apply to be a waitress, her air of defiance suggesting to Lucy that Bridget's mother hadn't liked the idea of her working. Bridget was resisting the idea of staying close to home after graduation and doing her first two years at the community college in Port Angeles rather than going away. Was she trying to earn enough to pay a significant part of her own expenses? If so, there was no doubt whose side Lucy was on.

Still, she wished every decision she made didn't have

family repercussions. The tiniest stone spread ripples of gossip, hurt feelings, righteous indignation. That was the problem with having such a large family who all lived so close by. Making a face, Lucy thought wistfully, *Why can't one side or the other live in Minneapolis or Houston instead? Anywhere but here?*

Dad's family, by preference. His sister, her Aunt Lynn, was a particular trial. Come to think of it, Lucy didn't like most of her cousins on Dad's side, either.

The trouble was, Dad had a sister and a brother, who had kids, all of whom had already started families of their own. Mom had two sisters, and *they* had kids, and... Aagh! There was a reason Lucy had yearned to leave Middleton for most of her life.

She ran the cash register as the full restaurant gradually emptied, and by the time she thought to look at the small table in the bow window, it was empty. Erin, another employee, was starting to clear it, and Lucy was disappointed to see that the soup bowl was half-full, and Miss Browning hadn't even finished her scone.

Oh, dear, she thought. If only the hat lady would fill up when she was here. Or take leftovers in a doggie bag. She accepted invitations to dine, but wouldn't come more than a couple of times a week. Lucy knew that she did get food elsewhere. George, down at Safeway, saw to it that expired canned goods and slightly wilted produce got set outside the back door when the hat lady's route took her that way. And Winona Carlson, who ran the Pancake Haus out by the highway, fed her breakfast at least another couple of days a week. Still... When Lucy thought about the hat lady—gentle, whimsical, yet somehow sad—she worried.

Today, though, she was too busy to do more than shake her head and feel slightly guilty that she hadn't made time to sit down, if only for a minute or two. Then she went back to work in the kitchen, prepping for dinner.

Hands busy, she let her mind wander. That one achingly perceptive look from the hat lady set her to analyzing why she'd felt so down lately.

Of course, she knew in part: this wasn't the life she'd dreamed of having. Like her niece Bridget, she'd been sure she would leave Middleton behind and never be back except for visits. But after college she'd let herself get enveloped again by family. First a job at the café, the chance to be creative in the kitchen and the pleasure of seeing how her food was received. Wan lettuce and all-American comfort foods were gradually replaced by wraps, spinach and romaine salads and her signature soups. When the opportunity to buy the café came up, she'd still told herself this didn't have to be permanent. She'd improve business and make a profit when she sold the café in turn. Perhaps she could start a restaurant in Seattle or San Francisco, or get a job as an executive chef.

Her hands went still as her chest filled with something very like panic. All of a sudden she had a terrible urge to turn the sign on the door to Closed, scrap preparation for dinner and just…run away.

Lucy grimaced. She was far too responsible to do any such thing. Okay, then; why not put the café up for sale and use the proceeds to travel for a couple of years? Give in to all the yearnings that made her so restless. Spend a year traveling between hostels in…Romania. Or Swaziland. Or…

The hat lady's face popped into her mind, and a smile curved her mouth. *England. How silly of me! Of course it has to be the British Isles.* Images of thatched roofs and hedgerows, church spires and castle towers rose before her mind's eye. Perhaps she would bike between villages, staying as long as she chose in each. She'd have to start over financially when she came home, if she ever came home, but she was young. At least she'd have lived a little before she settled into being a small-town businesswoman.

Elizabeth Barrett Browning would certainly approve.

Only a pair of tourists sat in front eating pie in the late afternoon when the front door opened so precipitously, the bell rattled and banged against the glass. Startled, Lucy let the dough she'd been kneading drop and peered over the divider between the kitchen and dining room.

It was George who'd rushed in, expression distraught. George, fifty-five and counting the years until retirement, who Lucy had believed had only one speed: measured, deliberate. George, who now let the door slam behind him with a bang.

"Lucy! Did you hear?"

Hands covered with flour, she used her shoulder to push the swinging door open and go into the dining room. She was vaguely aware that both the tourists and gray-haired Mabel, who was wiping down tables, had turned to stare. "Hear? Hear what?"

"The hat lady was hit crossing the highway." His eyes were red-rimmed and he looked as if he might cry. "She was pushing her shopping cart, and apparently didn't look. God." He rubbed a hand over his face. "She's not dead, but it doesn't sound good."

"Did they take her to the hospital?"

He nodded.

"But…she doesn't have insurance."

A silly thing to say, since the hat lady also didn't have a name. Not a real name, one that was her own for sure.

"I didn't hear anybody quibbling." So he'd been to the hospital.

Lucy took a deep breath. "I'll get over there as soon as I can."

He nodded and left, perhaps to spread the word further.

Lucy called for Mabel to take over the dough, and remembered another line written by Elizabeth Barrett Browning, whose poetry she, too, had loved, back when she was romantic and firmly believed her path would take her far from too familiar Middleton.

Life, struck sharp on death,
Makes awful lightning.

ADRIAN RUTLEDGE was immersed in the notes his associates had made on legal precedents for a complex case that would be coming to trial next month when his phone rang. He glanced at it irritably; he'd asked Carol, his administrative assistant, not to interrupt him until his three o'clock appointment.

He reached for the phone immediately, however. She wouldn't have bothered him without good reason.

"Yes?"

She cleared her throat. "Mr. Rutledge, there's a woman here who doesn't have an appointment."

His eyebrows rose. People without appointments rarely bothered a partner in a rarified Seattle law firm.

If they did, Carol was quite capable of sending them on their way.

"She says it's about your mother."

"My mother," he repeated. He felt as if he were sounding out a word in Farsi or Mandarin, a language utterly foreign to him. Yeah, he knew what a mother was; yeah, he'd had one, but at this moment he couldn't picture her face.

"Yes, sir." Carol's generally crisp tones were hesitant.

"What about my mother?" he asked.

She cleared her throat again. "This woman…ah, Ms. Peterson, says she's in the hospital and needs you."

In the hospital? That meant…she was *alive?* His heart did a peculiar stutter. Adrian had assumed she was dead. Maybe preferred thinking she was.

Oh, hell, he thought in disgust, this was probably some kind of hoax. Still, he didn't seem to have any choice but to hear her out. "Send her in," he ordered, and hung up.

The wait seemed long. When the door did open, he saw Carol first, elegant in a sleek black suit and heels that made the most of her legs. He quit noticing his administrative assistant the moment the other woman walked in. Nor was he aware of Carol quietly closing the door behind her. He couldn't take his eyes from this unexpected visitor.

He guessed her age as late twenties. Lacking the style of an average urban high schooler, she was as out of place as a girl from small-town Iowa wandering into the big city for the first time. Of middle height and slender, she wore a dress, something flowery that came nearly to her knees. Bare legs, flat shoes. Her hair, a soft, mousy brown, was parted in the middle and partially clipped back. He doubted she wore any makeup at all, which was too bad; she might be beautiful after a few hours at a good salon. It was her eyes that he reacted to, despite himself. Huge and blue, they devoured his face as she crossed the room, the intensity enough to make him shift in his seat.

Adrian had never seen her in his life, and couldn't imagine how she'd found him.

Showing no emotion, he held out a hand. "I'm Adrian Rutledge."

She shook with utter composure. "My name's Lucy Peterson."

"Ms. Peterson." He gestured at a chair. "Please. Have a seat."

"Thank you." She sat, smoothing her skirt over her knees.

She didn't look like his mother. He realized that had been his first fear; that he had an unknown half sister. Not that children always did look like their parents, he reminded himself. The possibility was still on the table.

"What can I do for you?"

"I assume you know nothing of your mother's whereabouts."

Dark anger rose in him at this blunt beginning. Who the hell was she to sit in judgment on him? And she was, he could tell, despite her careful tone.

"And you know this because…?"

"I live over on the peninsula. Your mother has been homeless in my town for the past ten years. I'm reasonably certain no family has visited her or offered any support."

What in hell?

Adrian sat back in his leather desk chair. After a moment, he said, "You're correct in thinking I have no contact with my mother. But tell me just why it is that you believe some homeless woman is my mother? Did she give you my name?"

This Lucy Peterson shook her head. "No. After she was in the accident, I searched her things. It wasn't easy." She seemed to assume he'd care. "She had a shopping cart, but she also had several stashes around town. She liked clothes. And hats. Especially hats. We called her the hat lady." She paused, as if embarrassed.

Between one blink and the next, Adrian saw a park, maybe—lots of lawn, flowering trees in the background. His mother barefoot and twirling, a cotton skirt swirling bell-like, her arms flung out in exuberance. She was laughing; he could almost hear the laugh, openly joyous. And see the hat, broad-brimmed and encircled with flowers. The image seemed skewed, as if he'd been dizzy, and he suspected he might have been twirling, too.

He stamped down on the memory. Unclenching his jaw, he asked hoarsely, "What did you find?"

In answer, she bent to open the purse she'd set at her feet and removed a white envelope. "A very old driver's license," she said, and handed it to him.

In shock, he stared at his mother's face. She was so pretty. He'd forgotten. Department of Motor Vehicles photos were usually god-awful, the equivalent of mug shots, but hers was the exception. A soft smile curved her mouth, although her eyes looked sad. Honey-blond, wavy hair was cut, flapper style, at chin length. She'd had beautiful cheekbones, a small, straight nose and that mouth, a cupid's bow.

He forced himself to read the information: Elizabeth H. Rutledge, the expiration date—one year after she disappeared from his life—and the basic stats, hair blond, height five foot five, weight 118, eyes blue.

Not as blue as Lucy Peterson's, he thought involuntarily, looking up.

He had no idea what his face showed, but those eyes were filled with compassion as she handed him something else. As he accepted it involuntarily he looked down, and experienced a spasm of agony. The photograph had faded and cracked, but he remembered the moment. They had dressed for church, and his grandmother had snapped it. His father was tall and stern, but his arm wrapped his wife protectively. She wore a pretty, navy-blue dress with a wide red belt, and on her head was a hat, this one a small red cloche with only a feather decorating it. And he…he stood beside her, his arm about her waist, her hand resting on his shoulder. He remembered feeling proud and mature and yet filled with some anxiety, as though there had been a family quarrel earlier. He might have been seven or eight, his dark hair slicked firmly into place, the suit and white shirt and tie a near match to his father's. He could just make out the house behind them, the one in Edmonds where they'd lived, painted sunny yellow with white trim, the yard brimming with flowers.

He was speechless. His mother had left him, and never once in all the intervening years made contact, yet she'd kept and treasured this photo?

Not just the photo—Lucy was handing over yet one more memento, this one made of red construction paper. On the front was a drawing, the next best thing to stick figures, an adult and a child seemingly holding hands. A woman, because she wore a skirt. His mother, because she also wore a hat festooned with…God. Those had to be flowers. And beneath, in big, uneven letters that suggested he might have been in kindergarten or first grade, it said "Mom and me."

As if through a time warp, he heard his own voice say, "Mom and me are going to the park." *And don't try to stop us,* the defiance in the words suggested. As if he had an eye pressed to a kaleidoscope that spun dizzily, he saw scene after scene, all accompanied by his voice, younger, older, in between, saying, "Mom and me are gonna…" She was his playmate, his best friend, his charge. He stayed close to her. He took care of her.

Until she disappeared, the summer he wasn't home to take care of her.

"God," he whispered, and let the card fall to the desk. He bowed his head and pinched the bridge of his nose.

Lucy Peterson sat silent, letting him process all of this.

He felt as if he'd just been in a car accident. No warning; another vehicle running a red light, maybe, slamming into his. This was the moment of silence afterward, when he sat stunned, trying to decide if he was injured, knowing he'd start hurting any minute.

He lifted his head and said fiercely, "And you know this…homeless person is her? Elizabeth Rutledge."

Lucy bit her lip and nodded. "I had no idea, until I found the driver's license. I guessed her name was Elizabeth. She always went by some variant of it. But that's all any of us knew."

"She didn't tell you her *name?*"

"She…took on different names. All famous people,

or fictional ones. I think she believed she was them, for a while. I never saw the moment of transition. One day she'd be Elizabeth Bennett, from *Pride and Prejudice,* you know, and then Queen Elizabeth. Not the first," she added hastily. "She said Queen Bess was bloodthirsty. Elizabeth the second."

"I'm surprised she wasn't the Queen Mother," he said involuntarily.

"Because of the hats? But she wasn't an Elizabeth, and your mother didn't take on any persona that wasn't."

Abruptly he heard the verb tense she was using. *Took on. She believed.* Not *takes on,* or *believes.*

"I thought you said she was in the hospital."

She looked startled. "I did."

"You're talking about her as if she's dead."

"Oh." Once again she worried the lip, as if she often did. "I'm sorry. It's just…the prognosis isn't very good, I'm afraid. She's in a coma."

When he asked, she told him what had happened. That she'd been pushing her shopping cart across the highway, probably on her way to the Safeway store on the other side. The car that hit her had been going too fast, the police had determined, but she had likely been in her own world and hadn't looked before starting across, either.

"She was sent flying twenty feet. The cart…" She swallowed. "It was flattened. Her things strewn everywhere. That was over a week ago. She hasn't stirred since. There was swelling in her brain at first, of course, but they drilled into her skull to relieve it. Which sounds gruesome, but…"

He nodded jerkily. "I understand."

"The thing is, until now it never occurred to any of us to try to find her family. I'm ashamed that it didn't. We tried to take care of her, as much as she'd let us, but… She was just a fixture. You know? Now I wonder, if I'd pushed her—"

"If she didn't know who she was, how could she tell you?"

"But she must have remembered something, or she wouldn't have held on to those. Oh, and these rings." She took them from the envelope and dropped them into his outstretched hand.

A delicate gold wedding band, and an engagement ring with a sizeable diamond. Undoubtedly his father's choice. Adrian remembered it digging into his palm when he grabbed at his mother's hand.

He wanted to feel numb. "She could have sold these."

"It wasn't just the rings she was holding on to," Lucy said softly, her gaze on them. "She was holding on to who she was. On to *you*."

"I haven't heard from her in twenty-three years." He felt sick and angry, and the words were harsh.

"Do you think she didn't love you?"

He hated seeing the pity in her eyes. Jaw tightening, he said, "Let's get back to facts. Where is she?"

"Middleton Community Hospital. Middleton's not far off Highway 101, over the Hood Canal Bridge."

He nodded, already calculating what he had to cancel. Of course, he'd want to transfer her to a Seattle hospital rather than leave her in the hands of a small-town doctor, but first he had to get over there and assess the situation.

"I was hoping you might come," Lucy said.

Glancing at the clock, he said, "I'll be there by evening. I have to clear my schedule and pack a few things."

He saw the relief on her face, and knew she hadn't been sure how he'd react. He might not be willing to drop everything and come running, had his mother walked out on her family for another man, say, or for mercenary reasons. As it was, he might never know why she'd gone, but it was clear she was mentally ill. His childish self had known she wasn't quite like other mothers. Even then, she'd battled depression and a tendency to hear voices and see people no one else saw.

Schizophrenia, he'd guessed coldly as an adult, and still guessed. Her reasons for whatever she'd done were unlikely to make sense to anyone but her. There might be nothing he could do for her now, but she was his obligation and no one else's.

He rose to his feet. "You can tell her doctor to expect me."

She nodded, thanked him rather gravely, and left, apparently satisfied by the success of her errand.

He called Carol and told her to cancel everything on his book for the rest of the week. Then, with practiced efficiency, he began to pack his briefcase. Hospital visiting hours would be limited. Once he'd seen the doctor, he could get plenty done in his hotel room.

CHAPTER TWO

ADRIAN HAD NEVER taken a journey during which he'd been less eager to reach his destination.

Instead of turning on his laptop to work while he waited in line for the ferry, he brooded about what awaited him in Middleton.

He knew one thing: other people besides Lucy Peterson would be looking at him with silent condemnation as they wondered how a man misplaced his mother.

Yeah, Dad, how did *you lose her?*

Or had he discarded her? In retrospect, Adrian had often wondered. He loved his grandparents, but he hadn't wanted to spend an entire summer in Nova Scotia without his mother. Some part of him had known she needed him. Years later, as he grew older, he'd realized that his father had arranged the lengthy visit so that no fiercely protective little boy would be around to object or ask questions when Elizabeth was sent away.

Supposedly she'd gone to a mental hospital. His father had never taken Adrian to visit, probably never visited himself. Perhaps a year later he'd told Adrian that she had checked herself out of the hospital.

With a shrug, he said, "Clearly, she didn't want to get well and come home. I doubt we'll ever hear from her again."

Subject dismissed. That was the last said between them. The last that ever would be said; his father had died two years ago in a small plane crash.

Adrian moved his shoulders to release tension. Let the good citizens of Middleton stare; he didn't care what they thought. He was there to claim his mother, that was all.

What if he didn't recognize her? If he gazed at the face of this unconscious woman and couldn't find even a trace of the mother he remembered in her?

Ask for DNA testing, of course, but was that really what worried him? Or did his unease come from a fear that he wouldn't recognize her on a more primitive level? Shouldn't he *know* his mother? What if he saw her and felt nothing?

He grunted and started the car as the line in front of him began to move. God knows he hadn't felt much for his mother. Why would he expect to, for a woman he hadn't seen in twenty-three years?

Usually, he would have stayed in his car during the crossing and worked. But his mood was strange today, and he knew he wouldn't be able to concentrate. Instead, he followed most of the passengers to the upper deck, then went outside at the prow.

This early in the spring, the wind on the sound had a bite. He hadn't bothered to change clothes at home, had stopped at his Belltown condominium only long enough to throw what he thought he'd need into a suitcase. He buttoned his suit jacket to keep his tie from whipping over his shoulders, leaned against the railing and watched the gulls swoop over the ferry and the late-afternoon sunlight dance in shards off the choppy waves.

Why would his mother have chosen Middleton? Adrian wondered. How had she even found it? It was barely a dot on the map, likely a logging town once upon a time. Logging had been the major industry over here on the Olympic Peninsula until the forests had been devastated and hard times had come. Tourism had replaced logging on much of the peninsula, but what tourist would seek out Middleton, for God's sake? It wasn't on Hood Canal or the Strait of Juan de Fuca to the north. It was out in the middle of goddamn nowhere.

Why, Mom? Why?

He drove off the ferry at Winslow, on the tip of Bainbridge Island, then followed the two-lane highway that was a near straight-shot the length of the island, across the bridge and past the quaint town of Poulsbo. From then on, civilization pretty much disappeared but for a few gas stations and houses. Traffic was heavy, with this a Friday, so he couldn't eat up the miles the way he'd have liked to. No chance to pass, no advantage if he'd been able to. He crossed the Hood Canal Bridge, the water glittering in the setting sunlight. Summer homes clung like barnacles along the shore. Then forest closed in, second-growth and empty of any evidence of human habitation.

Reluctance swelled in him and clotted in his chest. A couple of times he rubbed his breastbone as if he'd relieve heartburn. The light was fading by the time he spotted the sign: Middleton, 5 Miles.

He was the only one in the line of traffic to make the turn. And why would anyone? Along with distaste for what lay ahead came increasing bafflement at his mother's choice. How had she even gotten here? Did the

town boast a Greyhound station? Had she gone as far
as her money held out? Stabbed her finger at a map? Or
had some vagary of fate washed her up here?

So close to Seattle, and yet she'd never tried to get
in touch with him.

So weirdly far from Seattle in every way that counted.

The speed limit dropped to thirty-five and he obe-
diently slowed as the highway—if you could dignify it
with that name—entered the outskirts. He saw the Safeway store almost immediately, and his foot lifted involuntarily from the gas pedal. Here. She was hit here.
Flung to one of these narrow paved shoulders. With
dark encroaching, he couldn't see where, or if any evidence remained.

Ahead, he saw the blue hospital sign, but some impulse made him turn the other direction, toward downtown. The Burger King on the left seemed the only
outpost of the modern world. Otherwise, the town he
saw under streetlights probably hadn't changed since the
1950s. There was an old-fashioned department store,
churches—he saw three church spires without looking
hard—pharmacy, hardware store. Some of the build-
ings had false fronts. All of the town's meager commerce seemed to lie along the one main street, except
for the Safeway.

A memory stirred in his head. Wasn't there a Middleton in Nova Scotia? Or a Middleburg, or Middle-
something? Had this town *sounded* like home to his
mother? Had she stayed, then, because it felt like home,
or because people here were good to her? Lucy Peterson
had expressed guilt that they hadn't done more, but
she'd obviously cared.

More than Elizabeth Rutledge's own family had.

His jaw muscles spasmed. If this woman was his mother, he'd have to tell his grandmother, who was frail but at eighty-two was still living in her house in the town of Brookfield in Nova Scotia. Would she be glad? Or grieve terribly to know what her daughter's life had been like?

He ran out of excuses not to go to the hospital after a half-dozen city blocks. There wasn't much to this town.

The hospital was about what he'd expected: two-story in the central block, with wings to each side. He parked and walked in the front entrance. The white-haired woman behind the desk looked puzzled when he asked for Elizabeth Rutledge. Then her face abruptly cleared.

"Oh! The hat lady! That's what Lucy said her name is. You must be the son." She scrutinized him with interest and finally disappointment. "You don't look like her, do you?"

With thinning patience, he repeated, "Her room number?"

She beamed, oblivious to his strained civility. "Two sixty-eight." She waved. "Just go right up the elevators there and then turn to your left."

Despite a headache, he forced himself to nod. "Thank you."

The elevator door opened as soon as he pushed the button. Not much business at—he glanced at his watch—7:13 in the evening. The doors opened again almost immediately, and he had no choice but to step out. He turned left, as ordered. A white-capped woman at the nurses' station was writing in a chart and didn't notice him when he passed.

Most of the doors to patient rooms stood ajar. TVs were on. Voices murmured. Laughter came from one room. From another, an ominous gurgling. In 264 a woman in a hospital gown was shuffling to the bathroom, her IV pole going with her, someone who might be a daughter hovering at her side. 266 was dark.

The door to 268 was wide open and the first bed was unoccupied. The curtain around the second bed was pulled, blocking his view. He heard a voice beyond the curtain; a nurse, maybe? Adrian stopped and took a deep breath. He couldn't understand why this was bothering him so much. Whether she was his mother or not, this woman was a stranger to him. An obligation. No more, no less.

He walked in.

Hooked to an IV and to monitors that softly beeped, a woman lay in the hospital bed.

One look, and he knew. Still as death, she was his mother. For a moment, he quit breathing.

Beside the bed, Lucy Peterson sat in a chair reading aloud.

Poetry, of all things.

She had a beautiful voice, surprisingly rich and expressive for a woman as subdued in appearance as she was. For a moment, he just listened, wondering if his mother heard at all. Was the voice a beacon, a golden glow, that led her back toward life? A puzzle that no longer made sense? Or was she no longer capable of understanding or caring?

However quiet his footfall, Lucy heard him and looked up, with a flash of those expressive blue eyes. She immediately closed the book without marking any place and set it on the table. "You're here."

She sounded ambivalent; pleased, maybe, in one way, less so in another. Glad he'd lived up to his word, but not sure she liked him?

He didn't care, although he was equally ambivalent about her presence. He wanted to focus on this woman in the bed—his mother—with no witnesses to his emotional turbulence. And yet he felt obscurely grateful that Lucy was here, a buffer. For once in his life, he needed her brand of simple kindness.

In response to her words, but ignoring her tone, he said, "Why so surprised? You beat me here."

"I didn't have to stop to pack."

He nodded. And made himself look fully at his mother's face.

After a long moment, he said, almost conversationally, "Do you know she's only fifty-six?"

"When I saw her driver's license."

"She looks…" He couldn't finish.

Very softly, Lucy said, "I thought she might be seventy."

His mother's face was weathered and lined far beyond her years, although the bone structure was the same. The slightly pointed chin, too, that had given her an elfin appearance. He'd noticed it most when her mood was fey, although it was nearly sharp now, whittled by hardship. Her hair was white, and thin. Her hands, still atop the coverlet, were knobbed with arthritis.

This was what a lifetime without adequate nutrition or medical care or beauty products did. Elizabeth Rutledge had been a beautiful woman. Now she was an old one.

Still, he devoured the sight of her face, the slightness of the body beneath the covers, the tired hands, with a hunger that felt bottomless. Inside, he was still the child who needed his mom and knew she needed him. He stepped forward, gripping the round metal railing on this side of the bed. The pain in his chest seared him.

"Mom." The word came out guttural, shocking him. He swallowed and tried again. "Mom. It's me. Adrian."

Of course, she didn't stir; no flicker of response twitched even an eyelid. She breathed. In and out, unaided, the only sign of life beyond the numbers on the monitor.

"I wish I'd known where you were. I would have come to get you a long time ago."

If he'd come two weeks ago, before the accident, would she have known him? She had changed, but at least in his memory she was an adult. How much did he resemble his ten-year-old self? Even his voice would still have been a child's. What were his chances now of getting through to her?

After a minute, in self-defense, he raised his gaze to Lucy Peterson, who watched him. "What was that you were reading?"

She glanced at the book. "Elizabeth Barrett Browning. I think I told you—" she bit her lip "—how much your mother liked her poetry."

So much, she'd believed she *was* Elizabeth Barrett Browning. And a host of other Elizabeths, real and imaginary. Just never herself, Elizabeth Hamlin Rutledge, once daughter of Burt and Lana Hamlin, then wife of Maxwell Rutledge and mother of Adrian.

Perhaps when he went away that summer and let go of his grip on her hand, she'd forgotten who she was. Had she lost herself that long ago?

"I wish I knew..." he murmured, unsure what he wished. For the true story of that summer, and the year that followed? To find out what happened after, how she'd washed up here, how she had come to grasp for identities that had only a given name in common with her true self? All of the above?

"Ah," said a voice behind him. "You must be the son."

Adrian let go of the railing and turned. The doctor who'd entered was an elderly man, short and cherubic, head bald but for a white tonsure. He wore a lab coat open over a plaid golf shirt. Smiling, he held out his hand and they shook.

Then he looked past Adrian and shook his head in disapproval. "Lucy, you're back. You know, she won't float away if you go home and watch a sitcom, take a long bath, get to bed early."

Adrian supposed that was a good way to describe his childish fears about his mother: that she might float away if he let go. There had always been something insubstantial about her, not quite anchored to the here and now.

Lucy smiled, but said, "I didn't want Mr. Rutledge to feel abandoned."

Adrian knew vaguely that women like this did exist—caretakers, nurturers. Or perhaps he was jumping to a conclusion where she was concerned. Maybe it was only his mother who inspired this fierce need to protect.

"It sounds as if Ms. Peterson went to a lot of effort to locate me," he said.

"And thank God she succeeded. Ah…I'm Ben Slater."

"I appreciate your taking care of her, Doctor. I'm hoping you can tell me more about what's going on with my mother so that I can make decisions about her care."

"I haven't been able to do much. The truth is, with brain injuries we're most often left waiting. However much we learn, there's more we don't know. Someone who got a minor knock on the head dies, someone who falls ten stories to the sidewalk barely has a headache. I wish I could tell you how much damage she sustained, but I can't. She has a broken hip and ribs as well as some internal bleeding from the impact of the car, but the real problem is that she was lifted in the air and flung a fair distance onto the pavement. She struck her head hard. We did relieve some swelling in the brain, but it's subsided satisfactorily. She may yet simply open her eyes and ask where she is."

And she may not. Adrian had no trouble hearing what Slater didn't say.

On the other hand, how many head injuries had this small-town doc actually seen? What was he? Their trauma specialist? They did have an E.R., so they must have a specialist.

"Has she been seen by a neurologist?" Adrian asked, knowing the answer.

"Oh, I'm a neurosurgeon," Dr. Slater said cheerily. "Retired, of course. My wife was from Middleton, and we always intended to retire here. But I still do some consulting."

This fat little guy in the plaid shirt was a *neurosurgeon?* Was that possible?

Barely managing to suppress his you've-got-to-be-kidding reaction, Adrian asked, "Where did you work?"

"Ended up at Harborview in Seattle. I was on the University of Washington faculty."

Adrian's preconceptions didn't quite vanish—it was more like watching a piece of paper slowly burn until only grey, weightless ash hung insubstantially in the air.

His mother wasn't being cared for by some small-town practitioner who'd probably been in the bottom quarter of his class. By bizarre chance, her doctor might be one of the most highly qualified specialists in the country.

"My mother is fortunate you happened to be here."

"She would have been if I could fix her. I can't."

"And you don't think anyone can."

He shook his head, his gaze resting on his patient's face. "It's up to her now. Or to God, if you believe. Lucy—" he smiled at the young woman "—may do more good by sitting here talking and reading to your mother than I can with all the technology at my disposal."

Neurosurgeons were not known for their humility or fatalism. Adrian still had trouble believing in this one. But perhaps a lifetime of trying to salvage brain-damaged people made a man both fatalistic and humble.

Dr. Slater talked some more, about reflexes and brainwaves, but Adrian had begun to feel numb. The guy noticed, and abruptly stopped. "We should talk about this tomorrow. I understand you haven't seen your mother in years. You must be in shock."

"You could say that," Adrian admitted.

"Lucy," the doctor said briskly, "did you make arrangements for him for the night?"

Rebellion stirred, but honestly Adrian hoped she had a better suggestion than the crummy motel with kitchenettes he'd seen half a mile back.

"Yes, Sam's holding a room for him," she said. "If that's all right," she added, looking at him.

"Sam?"

"My sister Samantha. She owns a bed-and-breakfast. It's very nice."

He nodded. "Then thank you."

"And unless you had dinner on the way…" Seeing his expression, she said firmly, "We'll stop at the café on the way. It's late, but we'll come up with something."

"Good." The doctor patted her hand, shook Adrian's, said "I'll see you tomorrow," then departed.

Lucy picked up her book and started toward the door in turn. "I'll leave you alone with your mother for a few minutes. Just come on out when you're ready."

He was ready now, but in the face of her faith that he wanted to commune with this unconscious woman, he once again stepped to the bedside and looked down at her face. The resemblance to the mother he remembered was undeniably there, but in a way that made him uncomfortable. Age aside, it was like the difference between a living, breathing person and an eerily real cast of that person at a wax museum. He might as well have been standing here looking at his mother's body at the morgue.

But he knew why Lucy had been reading aloud. The silence had to be filled. "It's Adrian," he said tentatively. "I missed you. I didn't know what happened. Why you went away. I still don't know. I'd like to hear about it, when you wake up."

He couldn't quite bring himself to touch her. Not surprising, given that he wasn't much for hugs and hand-holding. Maybe he was afraid he'd find her hands to be icy cold.

"Well. Ah. I'll be back in the morning. I'll probably make arrangements to move you to Seattle, where you can be close to me."

An uneasy sense that she might, in fact, not like his plan stirred in him, but what the hell else was he supposed to do? Leave her here and drive back and forth for obligatory visits? Did they even have a long-term nursing facility here, assuming that's what she required?

He cleared his throat, said, "Good night," and escaped.

LUCY WAS PRETTY sure she didn't like Adrian Rutledge, but she was prepared to feel sorry for him when he walked out of his mother's hospital room. This had to be hard for him.

However, his expression was utterly composed when he appeared. "You needn't feel you have to feed me. If you just want to tell me the options and directions to the bed-and-breakfast."

"I have to stop by the café and see how they're doing without me," she explained. "I own it. Friday evening is one of our busiest times. I'm usually there. I may not have time to sit down with you."

He didn't look thrilled to be going anywhere with her, but finally nodded. "Fine. Should I follow you?"

"My car's right out front. Yours, too, I assume?"

He nodded again, the motion a little jerky. Maybe he wasn't as cold as he seemed. Lucy tried to imagine how disoriented he must feel by now.

Be charitable, she reminded herself. *For the hat lady's sake, if not his.*

Lisa Enger, the night nurse, greeted them. "I'll keep a good eye on her," she promised.

They rode down in the elevator silently, both staring straight ahead like two strangers pretending the other wasn't there. Lucy was usually able to chat with just about anybody, but she was pretty sure he wouldn't welcome conversation right now. Not until they were out in the parking lot did she speak.

"There's my car."

He nodded and pointed out his, a gray Mercedes sedan.

"I'll come down your row."

"All right."

Her small Ford Escort felt shabbier when the Mercedes fell in behind it, and she sympathized. She felt plain and uninteresting in his presence, too. She and her car had a lot in common.

He parked beyond her on Olympic Avenue half a block from the café, then joined her on the sidewalk.

"I'm sorry you had to take the day off to drive all the way to Seattle."

"Would you have believed a word I said if I'd just called?"

He was silent until they reached the door. "I don't know."

Well, at least he was honest.

He held open the door for her. Slipping past him, Lucy was more aware of him than she'd let herself be to this point. She'd known he was handsome, of course, and physically imposing. That his thick, dark hair was expensively cut, his charcoal suit probably cost more than she spent on clothes in a year and that his eyes were a chilly shade of gray. She refused to be intimidated by him. But just for a second, looking at his big, capable hand gripping the door and feeling the heat of his body as she brushed him, she felt her heart skip a beat.

He'd definitely be sexy if only he were more likeable. If he didn't look at her as if she were the janitor who'd quit scrubbing the floor long enough to try to tell him his business.

She grimaced. Okay, that might be her own self-esteem issues talking. He probably looked down on everyone. It was probably an advantage in corporate law, turning every potential litigant into a stuttering idiot.

Following her into the restaurant, he glanced around, apparently unimpressed by the casual interior and the half-dozen remaining diners.

"Your mother ate here a couple of times a week," she told him.

His eyebrows rose. "She had money...?"

Lucy shook her head. "She was my guest."

A muscle ticked in his cheek. "Oh."

For a moment Lucy thought he would feel compelled to thank her. A surprisingly fierce sense of repugnance filled her. Who was he to speak for the mother he didn't even know?

She hastily grabbed a menu and led him to the same table where his mother always sat, right in front of the window. "I'll be back to take your order as soon as I check in the kitchen."

It was easy to pretend she was immersed in some crisis and send Melody out to take his order instead. Once his food was delivered, Lucy stole surreptitious looks as he ate. She was pleased to see that he actually looked startled after the first spoonful of curried lentil soup, one of her specialties and personal favorites. He'd probably expected something out of a can.

Melody was prepared to close up for her, so once she saw him decline dessert, Lucy went back out to reclaim him. Without comment she took his money, then said, "I'm ready to go if you'd like to follow me again."

A hint of acerbity crept into his tone. "Do you think I'd get lost?"

"I pass Sam's place on my way home. I won't stop."

He nodded. "Then thank you."

It was getting harder for him to squeeze those *thank-yous* out, Lucy judged. Clearly, he wasn't in the habit of being in anyone's debt.

Once again he held open the door for her, the courtesy automatic. At least he was polite.

Outside, she said, "It's called Doveport Bed and Breakfast. You'll see it on the right, about half a mile from here. There's a sign out front."

He nodded, pausing on the sidewalk while she opened her car door and got in. More good manners, Lucy realized; in Seattle, a woman might be in danger if she were alone even momentarily on a dark street. Maybe his mother had instilled some good qualities in him, before she disappeared from his life.

However *that* happened.

Her forehead crinkled. How old had he been when his parents divorced, or his mother went away? Twenty-three years ago, he'd said. Surely he wasn't more than in his mid-thirties now. So he probably wasn't even a teenager when he lost her.

Was he bitter at what he saw as abandonment? Lucy hadn't been able to tell. Since she'd handed him the driver's license and photo in his office, he'd seemed more stunned than anything. She'd almost had the sense he was sleepwalking, that he hadn't yet figured out how to react. At least, she hoped that's what he was doing, and that he wasn't always so unemotional. Because if he was, she hated to think of the hat lady consigned to his care.

Lucy made sure the lights of his car were right behind her until she reached Sam's B and B. His headlights swept the sign, and his turn signal went on. She accelerated and left him behind, wondering if she'd arrive at the hospital tomorrow and find he had already made plans to have his mother moved to Seattle.

She shuddered to think of the gentle, confused hat lady waking to the stern face of this son she didn't remember, her bewildered gaze searching for other, familiar faces.

Unhappily she wondered if finding him had been the right thing to do after all.

CHAPTER THREE

STRANGELY, WHEN Adrian lay in bed that night, he kept thinking about Lucy Peterson instead of his mother. Maybe he was practicing avoidance. He didn't know, but he was bothered by the fact that he didn't understand her. He prided himself on being able to read people. The ability to anticipate reactions made him good at his job.

He'd long since learned that self-interest was paramount in most people. But if a single thing Lucy had done for his mother—and now for him—helped her in any way, he couldn't see it. So what motivated her? Why had she noticed his mother in the first place? Downtown Seattle was rife with homeless people, sleeping in doorways, curled on park benches, begging on corners, huddling from the rain in bus shelters. To most people, they fell somewhere between annoying and invisible. When had Lucy first stopped to talk to his mother? Offered her a meal?

Why had she cared so much that she'd been determined to find the confused old lady's family?

He kept puzzling it out and not arriving at any answers. That bugged him. Yeah, she might just be the nurturing kind. But even people like that didn't usually nurture a homeless person. Anyway, she wasn't a completely soft touch, ready to expect the best of everyone. She'd certainly made a judgment about him before she even met him. She was doing her best for him because of his mother, but she didn't like having to do it.

That stung, which bothered him, too. Why in hell would he care what a small-town café owner thought of him?

He shifted restlessly in bed, picturing the way she looked at him, her eyes seeming to dissect him.

Adrian fell asleep eventually, but his dreams were uneasy and he jerked awake several times. The damn bed was too soft. The down pillows kept wadding into lumps beneath his head. Even the scent of potpourri in the room was unfamiliar and too sweet, slipping into his dreams.

He got up in the morning feeling jittery yet exhausted. The room was nice enough if you liked such things, he'd noted last night, and was decorated with obligatory old-fashioned floral wallpaper and antiques. He didn't much care, but was relieved to have his own bathroom. This morning, though, he walked into it and stopped dead, staring at the enormous, claw-footed tub.

"What the hell...?" His incredulous gaze searched the wall above, and returned to the faucet that didn't even have a handheld showerhead. He hated taking baths. All he wanted was a hard spray of hot water to bring him to his senses.

Given no choice, however, he took a hasty bath, got dressed and went downstairs to sample the breakfast.

If he had to sit at a common table, he'd head to town instead. Chatting over breakfast with complete strangers held no appeal. He'd find a diner if he had to drive to Sequim. Fortunately, the dining room held several tables. A family sat at one, a couple at another. He took a place as far from the others as he could get.

He hadn't paid much attention to his hostess last night, but this morning he studied her in search of a resemblance to her sister. They did both have blue eyes. Samantha Peterson was less striking but prettier. She wore her curly blond hair cut short and had a curvy figure. *She* didn't look at him as if he'd crawled out from a sewer drain. Instead, she chatted in a sunny way as she served thick slabs of French toast covered with huckleberries and powdered sugar, oatmeal and bacon that made his mouth water. It was the best breakfast he'd had in years; creativity in the kitchen obviously ran in the family.

Funny thing was, he knew he wouldn't remember her face two days from now. Her sister's would stick in his mind.

When Samantha paused to refill his coffee after everyone else had left the dining room, he asked, "Did you know my mother?"

"The hat lady? Sure, but not as well as Lucy. I'm not on her route, you know."

Puzzled, he asked, "Her route?"

"Um." As casually as if he'd invited her, she filled a second cup with coffee for herself and sat across from him. "Your mom had a routine. On a given day, you knew she'd have certain stops. The library on Mondays—they let her check out books even though she didn't have an address—the thrift shop Tuesdays, because they're closed Sunday and Monday and they always had new stuff then—"

"But she didn't have money."

She shrugged, the gesture both careless and generous. "It's run by the Faith Lutheran Church. They let her take whatever she wanted."

"Like hats," he reflected.

"Right. Another of her stops was Yvonne's Needle and Thread. Yvonne let her pick out trims, silk flowers, whatever, that she used to decorate the hats. The senior center has a pancake breakfast on Wednesday and a spaghetti dinner on Friday, and she was always at those. Lucy's twice a week, the Pancake Haus once a week, and so on."

What was with this town? Was every single citizen willing to give away whatever she'd wanted? Would any needy soul qualify, or just his mother? As a child he'd loved his mother, but he couldn't imagine that one vague old lady was that special.

"She loved garage sales," Samantha continued. "Oh, and rummage sales, like at one of the churches. During the season, she'd deviate from her usual route to take in any sales. She was always the first one there."

"She must have picked up the newspaper then, to read the classifieds."

"Probably," she said cheerfully.

Had his mother read the front page news? What did a woman who believed she was a nineteenth-century poet make of the presidential election or Mideast politics? Or did she skip anything that perplexed her?

Frowning, he asked, "Where did she sleep?"

"We're not quite sure. I offered her a room over the winter, but she wouldn't accept. I'm a little too far out from the center of town for her, I think. Father Joseph at Saint Mary's left a basement door unlocked for her when the weather was cold, and he says she did sleep there on a cot sometimes. And Marie at Olympic Motel says she'd occasionally stay there, too."

Adrian continued to grapple with the concept of an entire town full of do-gooders. "In other words, everybody knew her."

"Oh, sure." She smiled at him. "We did our best."

"I'm…grateful." The words were hard to say for a man who'd never in his life taken charity. Depending entirely on the kindness of strangers…he couldn't imagine.

No—maybe not strangers. She'd stayed here in Middleton long enough that she'd been theirs, in a sense. Lucy Peterson clearly felt proprietary.

Adrian discovered he didn't like the idea that every shopkeeper in this miserable town knew his mother, and he didn't.

Samantha waved off his gratitude. "Oh, heavens! We loved her."

There it was again, that past tense. Nobody expected her to survive. Or perhaps they assumed he'd take care of her now, as, of course, he intended to do.

He drained his coffee and made his excuses. Back in his room, he sat at the small desk and took out his cell phone. It was early enough he got through to an old friend.

Tom Groendyk and he had shared an old house in the U district through grad school. Tom was an orthopedic surgeon now at Swedish Medical Center, having left the area for his internship and residency but coming home two years ago.

"Hey. I have a favor to ask of you," Adrian said, after brief greetings. "You heard of a neurosurgeon named Ben Slater?"

"Are you kidding?" Tom laughed. "The guy looks like Santa Claus and grades like Scrooge."

"Is he any good?"

"Only the best. Hell of a teacher, and hell of a surgeon from what I hear." His voice sharpened. "Why? Is there something you haven't told me?"

Adrian and Tom played racquetball once a week, had dinner or met for drinks every couple of weeks. Tom hadn't married, either, although he was seeing a woman pretty seriously right now.

Adrian wouldn't have told many other people, but Tom did know some of his history. "I'm over on the peninsula," he said. "My mother has showed up."

There was a momentary silence. "Showed up?"

"She's apparently mentally ill. She's been homeless. Nobody knew who she was until she got hit by a car. When they searched her stuff, they found an old driver's license and tracked me down."

He didn't mention the photograph of his father, mother and him, or that Mother's Day card. He still wasn't ready to face the memories they had conjured up.

"If you're looking for the best to treat her, Slater's it," Tom said, adding, "But the guy's retired. I guess I could ask around and find out where he is, but I can give you some other names instead."

"He's here, believe it or not. Evidently his wife grew up here in Middleton, and they came back when he retired. He must have gotten bored. He's consulting now."

Tom let out a low whistle. "You got lucky then."

"He says there's nothing he can do for her. Either she comes out of the coma or she doesn't."

"So what are you asking me? Whether a different guy would tell you something else?"

Adrian squeezed the bridge of his nose. "Yeah. I guess that is what I'm asking. Should I get a second opinion?"

"If it were my mother," his friend said, "I wouldn't bother." However blunt the answer, his voice had softened. "Man, I'm sorry."

"Yeah. Thanks."

"So what are you going to do?"

"I don't know," Adrian admitted. "Go on over to the hospital, I guess. See how it goes over the next day or two. Then I suppose I'd better find someplace to move her to. I had Carol cancel my appointments through Tuesday. Fortunately, I didn't have anything earthshaking in the works."

"Yeah, listen, if there's anything I can do…"

"Thanks." He had to clear his throat. "I'll call." He hit End and sat there for a minute, his chest tight. What a bizarre conclusion to his childhood fantasies of finding his mom.

He felt no great eagerness to go sit at her bedside, but finally stood. He looked at his laptop and decided not to take it. Maybe this afternoon, if he went back to the hospital. He locked his room and left without seeing his hostess.

The hospital appeared even smaller and less prepossessing in daylight. He doubted it had sixty beds. It probably existed primarily as an emergency facility, given the recreational opportunities nearby in the Olympic National Park and on the water. Mountain climbers, hikers and boaters had plenty of accidents, and Highway 101, crowded with tourists, undoubtedly produced its share. Once stabilized, patients could be moved to a larger facility in Port Angeles or Bremerton if not across the sound to Seattle.

He knew his way today, and didn't pause at the information desk. This time a nurse intercepted him upstairs and said firmly, "May I help you?"

"I'm Elizabeth Rutledge's son."

"Oh! The hat lady." She flushed. "That is…"

He shook his head. "Don't worry about it."

"Dr. Slater stopped in briefly this morning. He said to tell you he'd be back this afternoon."

He nodded. "I thought I'd just sit with her for a while."

"We're so glad you're here. We're all very fond of her, you know."

Adrian studied the woman, graying and sturdy. "You knew her, too?"

"Not well, but my sister owns the Hair Do. Cindy washed and styled her hair regularly. Gave her perms every few months, too."

"Why?" Adrian asked bluntly.

She blinked. "Why?"

"Your sister is a businesswoman. Why would she give away her services to a homeless woman?"

She raised her eyebrows, her friendliness evaporating. "Lucy didn't say what you do for a living."

"I'm an attorney."

"Don't you do pro bono work?"

Everyone in the firm was required to handle the occasional pro bono case on a rotating schedule. "Yes," he admitted.

"What's the difference? Cindy likes your mom. Whenever I walked in, they'd be laughing like they were having the best time ever."

That was the payback? Laughter? And what the hell did a woman who couldn't remember who she was and who lived on the streets have to laugh about?

He went on to his mother's room, feeling the nurse's stare following him.

Somehow, he wasn't surprised to hear Lucy's voice when he walked in the open door.

She wasn't reading this morning, just talking.

"Yesterday, I saw some early daffodils opening. I know you'd have been as excited as I was. Well, they might have been narcissus or some species daffodil. Is there such a thing? These had orange centers and were small. But they were beautiful and bright." She paused, as if listening to an answer. When she went on, Lucy sounded regretful. "I wish I had time to garden. Every time I lug out the mower and tackle the lawn, I think about where I'd put flower beds. You know how much I'd like to grow old roses. I love to get out my books and think, too bad the China roses couldn't stand the cold here, but I'll definitely grow some of the really old ones. Rosamunde and Cardinal de Richelieu and Autumn Damask. Oh, and Celestial. And a moss rose. Have you ever seen one, with the fuzz all over the bud? I think they look fascinating. Even the names of the roses are beautiful. Fantin-Latour." She made every syllable sensuous. "Comte Chambord. Ispahan." She laughed. "Of course, I'm undoubtedly butchering them, since I don't speak French."

So she was sentimental. Why wasn't he surprised?

Adrian continued in, brushing the curtain as he rounded it. "Good morning."

She looked up, startled. "I didn't hear you coming."

Irrelevantly, he noticed what beautiful skin she had, almost translucent. Tiny freckles scattered from the bridge of her nose to her cheekbones. They hadn't been noticeable until now, with sunlight falling across her.

"I heard you talking about gardening."

Her cheeks pinkened, but Lucy only nodded. "Your mother told me spring was her favorite season. She loved to walk around town and look at everyone's gardens. Sometimes we dreamed together."

What a way to put it. Had he ever in his life dreamed together with anyone?

He knew the answer: with his mother.

Almost against his will, his gaze was drawn to her, looking like a marble effigy lying in that hospital bed. It was hard to believe this was the vivacious woman of his memory.

"We had a garden when I was growing up," he said abruptly. "In Edmonds. We didn't have a big yard, but it was beautiful. She spent hours out there every day on her knees digging in flower beds. I remember the hollyhocks, a row of them in front of the dining-room windows. Delphinium and foxgloves and climbing roses. Mom said she liked flowers that grew toward the sky instead of hugging the ground."

"Oh," Lucy breathed. "What a lovely thing to say."

"She talked like that a lot. My father would grunt and ignore her." Damn it, why had he said that? Adrian wondered, disconcerted. Reminiscing about his mother was one thing, about the tensions in his family another thing altogether.

"I'm sorry," Lucy said softly. Perhaps she saw his

face tighten, because instead of asking more about his father or when his mother had disappeared from his life, she said, "I thought about starting a small flower bed under my front windows this spring." Almost apologetically, she told him, "I don't have very much time to work in my yard. I wanted to take Elizabeth with me to the nursery to pick out the plants. She has such a good eye." Her hand crept onto the coverlet and squeezed the inert, gnarled hand of his mother. "I wish she'd wake up and say, 'When shall we go?'"

She sounded so unhappy, he thought with faint shock, *she loves Mom*. How did that happen?

"I'm surprised to see you here again this morning."

She wrinkled her nose. "Because Dr. Slater tried to bully me into staying away?"

His mouth twitched. He doubted Ben Slater knew how to bully anyone. Although... "I have a friend who took a class from him in med school. Tom says he's a tough grader."

"You checked up on him."

"Wouldn't you have?" he countered.

The pause was long enough to tell him how reluctant she was when she conceded, "I suppose so. Did he get a satisfactory rating?"

"A gold star. He's the best, Tom says."

"I could have told you that."

But he wouldn't have believed her. They both knew that.

When he didn't respond, she asked, "Have you made a plan yet?"

He looked back at his mother, watching as her chest rose and fell, the stirring of the covers so subtle he had to watch carefully to see it. "Move her to Seattle. What else can I do?"

As if he'd asked quite seriously, Lucy said, "Leave her here for now. Until Dr. Slater says she can go to a nursing home. And we even have one of those here in Middleton, you know."

God, he was tempted. Leave her to people who cared. Whose faces she'd recognized if she opened her eyes.

Abdicate.

He shook his head reluctantly. "I don't have time to be running over here constantly. And it sounds as if the chances are good she won't be waking up."

Lucy pinched her lips together. After a long time, she said, "I suppose that's true." She gazed at his mother, not him. "How soon will you be taking her?"

"I don't know. I'll get my assistant hunting for a place with an open bed."

Now she did turn a cool look on him. "Won't you want to check it out yourself?"

"Why do you dislike me?" he surprised himself by asking.

With a flash of alarm in her eyes, she drew back. "What would make you think—"

"Come on. It's obvious. You think I should have found her. Taken care of her."

Her chin rose fractionally. "I suppose I do."

Adrian shoved his hands in his pockets. "I did look for her some years back." He rotated his shoulders in discomfiture. "I suppose…not that hard. I thought she was dead."

Her brow crinkled. "Why?"

"Even as a kid, I knew there was something wrong with her. My father claimed she'd gone to a hospital to be treated. Then he told me she'd checked herself out because she didn't want to get well. I was young enough to believe that if she was alive, she wouldn't have left me."

She stared at him, and prompted, "Young enough to believe…? Does that mean, now that you're an adult, you don't have any trouble believing she'd ditch you without a second thought?"

God. He felt sick. That rich breakfast wasn't settling well in his stomach.

"Apparently she did," he said flatly.

He felt himself reddening as her extraordinary eyes studied him like a bug under a microscope.

She surprised him, though, by sounding gentle. "How old were you?"

His jaw tightened. "Ten."

"And you never saw her or heard from her again?"

He shook his head.

"How awful," she murmured, as if to herself. "Your father doesn't sound like a, um…"

"Warm man?" Irony in his voice, Adrian finished her thought. "No. You could say that."

"Have you told him…" She nodded toward the bed.

"He's dead."

"Oh." Compassion and an array of other emotions crossed her face, as if the sunlight coming through the window were suddenly dappled with small, fluttering shadows. "Do you have other family? I didn't think to ask if you had sisters or brothers."

Adrian shook his head. "Just me. Dad remarried, but as far as I know he and my stepmother never considered having kids."

She nodded, her gaze softer now, less piercing.

Without knowing why, he kept talking. "His parents are still alive. I'm not close to them." He hesitated. "My maternal grandmother is alive, too. I haven't told her yet."

"Oh! But won't she be thrilled?"

"I'm not so sure. She might have preferred to think her child was dead. To find out she didn't care enough to ever call home…" He shrugged.

"That's not fair! She forgot who she was!"

"But then *Maman* may feel she failed her in some way."

"Oh," Lucy said again. "*Maman?* Is that what you call her? Is she French?"

"French Canadian. She lives in Nova Scotia. That's where I was, with my grandparents, the summer my mother went away."

"What a sad story."

Oh, good. He'd gone from being a monster in her eyes to being pitiable. Adrian wasn't sure he welcomed the change.

When he said nothing, she flushed and rose to her feet. "I really had better go. I don't do breakfast, but it's time for me to start lunch." She hesitated. "If you'd like…"

What was she going to suggest? That she could feed him free of charge like she had his mother?

"Like?" he prodded, when she didn't finish.

"I was going to say that, after lunch, I could take an hour or two and introduce you to some of the people who knew your mother. They could tell you something about her life."

"Your sister started to."

He felt weirdly uncomfortable with the idea. But if his mother died without ever coming out of the coma, this might be the only way he'd ever find out who she'd become. Perhaps she'd even given someone a clue as to where she'd been in the years before she came to Middleton. He thought his grandmother, at least, would want to know as much as he could find out.

After a minute he nodded and said formally, "Thank you. I'd appreciate that."

Lucy smiled, lighting her pale, serious face, making her suddenly, startlingly beautiful in a way unfamiliar to him. Adrian's chest constricted.

He thought he took a step toward her, searching her eyes the way she often did his. Her pupils dilated as she stared back at him, her smile dying. He felt cruel when wariness replaced it.

She inched around him as if afraid to take her gaze from him, then backed toward the door. "I'll, um, see you later then? Say, two o'clock?"

"I'll come and eat lunch first." He paused. "Your soup was amazing."

The tiniest of smiles curved her lips again. "Wait until you taste my basil mushroom tomato soup."

His own mouth crooked up. "I'll look forward to it."

"Well, then…" She backed into the door frame and gave an involuntarily "umph" before she flushed in embarrassment, cast him one more alarmed look and fled.

He stood there by the curtain, the soft beep of the machines that monitored his mother's life signs in his ears, and wondered what in hell had just happened.

CHAPTER FOUR

THE CAFÉ WAS BUSY, which made it even more ridiculous that Lucy's heart insisted on skipping a beat every time the door opened and a customer entered. Was she excited at the prospect of spending more time with Adrian? Nervous about it? She didn't even know, but she didn't like reacting so strongly for no good reason at all.

For goodness' sake, he was going to eat lunch in the café! He'd eaten here last night. She planned to introduce him to a few people. He'd probably freeze her out in between stops. He was good at that.

Reason didn't seem to be helping. Something had changed between them this morning. He'd let her see the cracks in his facade of invulnerability. Well, he might not have *chosen* to show them, but they were there. He did hurt. This wasn't easy for him.

And he'd looked at her. Really looked, and maybe even liked what he'd seen. For just a moment, she'd seen something on his face that had stolen her breath and panicked her.

Common sense and reason did work to stifle any sense of expectation that he was suddenly, madly attracted to her. Okay, there might have been a brief flicker. But Lucy hated to think how she compared to the women he usually dated.

Her hands froze in the act of tossing salad in a huge bowl.

Dated? He could conceivably be married. When she researched him on the Internet before going over to Seattle that day, she didn't see anything to make her think he was, and he certainly hadn't mentioned a wife, as in, *My wife will visit any nursing homes my assistant finds,* which you'd think would be natural. But he was closemouthed enough that it was still possible.

And what difference did it make if he was? she asked herself with unaccountable depression. He was here in Middleton until Tuesday. Today was Saturday. Once he was gone, she'd probably get a nice note thanking her for taking care of his mother and that was it. Oh, and the chances were his assistant would've written the note. Wasn't that what assistants did?

Mabel stuck her head in the kitchen. "Erin just called in sick. She has a cold."

Lucy groaned. "Oh, no. Is it bad? Or an I-need-a-personal-day bug?"

"I didn't recognize her voice. It sounded like she has a doozy of a cold."

"Which we'd better not catch." Lucy frowned. "Okay. Why don't you call Bridget? I was going to hire her anyway. See if she can start tonight. She's spent enough time here she ought to be able to jump right in."

Mabel knew Lucy's aunt as well as Lucy did. "Beth doesn't want her to work."

"Yeah, I kinda suspected that. That's between them. I can't imagine she'd mind Bridget filling in."

"Probably not," Mabel conceded. She flapped a hand and retreated.

The bell on the door tinkled and Lucy's head snapped around. For the hundredth time.

It was him. He looked more human today, wearing running shoes, jeans and a V-neck blue jersey. Sexier, she realized, her pulse tap-dancing. Even his hair was a little disheveled.

Unlike last night, when his single glance around the café had been distant and even dismissive, today his gaze moved slowly and comprehensively from the old-fashioned, gilt-trimmed cash register and the jar of free mints to the artwork hanging on the walls, the windows with their red-checked curtains below lacy valances, the townsfolk and tourists nearly filling the tables and row of booths along the back wall and finally the cutout that allowed her to see him.

Their eyes met, and he nodded.

Lucy nodded, too, hastily, and ducked out of sight, her cheeks hot. He'd caught her gaping.

No, he hadn't. She'd glanced up because a patron had entered the café. She always kept half an eye on the front of the house even while she was cooking. Of course she did; it was her restaurant.

He had no reason to suspect he made her heart flutter, and she wouldn't give him any reason to.

What the heck. He'd probably be rude this afternoon to someone she really liked, and her heart would quit fluttering anyway.

When she looked out at the restaurant again, Mabel had seated him and he was studying a menu. Other people were covertly watching him. Lucy's cousin Jen was mur-

muring behind her hand to her best friend, Rhonda, who
owned the Clip and Curl, the competition to the Hair Do.
Rhonda had been heard saying disdainfully, "*I* wouldn't
have washed some homeless woman's hair. Imagine how
disgusting it must be." Lucy didn't like Rhonda, and Jen
wasn't her favorite relative, either. Jen, who liked feeling
important, would be telling all she knew about the rich
lawyer who was the homeless woman's son. The two
were probably both thrilled that he'd be ridding Middleton of the scourge of homelessness.

Jen had come by her tendency to gossip naturally. Her
mom was Lucy's Aunt Lynn. The one who was a trial.

Lucy had worked herself up to being annoyed
enough that she took off her apron and marched out,
ignoring Jen and Rhonda, straight to Adrian.

Maybe, if she were lucky, she'd start the whole family talking. Hadn't she wished for years that she'd done
something exciting enough to scandalize them?

"I'm glad you made it," she said.

He looked up from the menu. "You thought I was afraid
to show up?" Before she could answer, he said, "How's
the grilled-chicken sandwich with red-pepper aioli?"

"Fabulous," Lucy assured him. "Sam bakes the fo-
caccia bread for us."

"Ah." That apparently decided him, because he set
down the menu. "This is a family enterprise, huh?"

"No, it's mine, except that I've been buying baked
goods from Sam. And now we're talking about me
catering dinners for some special events she's thinking
of holding at the B and B. Like a mystery weekend. You
know." She paused. "Well, and I just added one of my
cousins to the waitstaff. Although her mom won't be

happy." Oh, brilliant. Like he'd care. "Are you ready for me to take your order?"

His eyes held a glint. "*Did* you think I wasn't going to show?"

"No. I doubt you ever back away from whatever you've decided is the best course."

Did that sound as rude to him as it had to her own ears?

His mouth twisted. "Oh, I have my cowardly impulses." Then his expression closed and he said, "I'd like the grilled-chicken sandwich and a cup of your soup."

"Anything to drink?"

"Just coffee."

"It'll be right out," she said, and went back to the kitchen.

Mabel was dishing up soup. Voice dry, she said, "Bridget squealed and said, 'I can start tonight? Awesome!'"

"She's young."

"She'll do fine," Mabel said comfortably. "If she's floundering, I'll stay late."

Lucy smiled at her. "Thank you. You're a lifesaver."

"What'd Mr. Attorney order?"

"Adrian." Lucy moderated a voice that had come out sharper than she'd intended. "His name is Adrian Rutledge."

Mabel's carefully plucked eyebrows rose. "Didn't mean to be insulting."

"It *sounded* insulting." Lucy sighed. "Forget it. Rhonda and Jen are out there whispering, and that got my back up."

"They get my back up every time they come in here. Don't worry." She nodded toward the front. "Are you getting his order?"

"Yes, and I'm going to take a couple of hours after the rush is over to introduce him to people who knew his mom. He wants to find out what he can about her."

"Uh-huh." Mabel's skepticism was plain, but she grabbed two salads and whisked out of the kitchen before Lucy could demand to know why she was hostile to Adrian.

Lucy did deliver his food, but she didn't have time to sit with him any more than she had with the hat lady the last time she'd come here. The better business was, the less time Lucy had to do anything but hustle. Between cooking and doing the ordering, she had precious few hours away from the café, and in some of those she kept the books, made deposits and created new recipes.

She *liked* cooking. She liked experimenting, and chatting with customers, and showing everyone she could succeed. But the responsibility of owning the place and having half a dozen other people's livelihoods depend on her was so overwhelming, she had no chance to even imagine what else she could do with her life. She hadn't been on a date in... Lucy had to count back. Four and a half months, and that was playing tennis at the club in Port Angeles and lunch afterward with Owen Marshall. And that hadn't been what you'd call a success. After watching him throw a temper tantrum when he lost a set to her, she hadn't hesitated to say no the next time he called.

Lately, no one else was asking, and it didn't appear likely anyone would in the near future. She knew every single guy in Middleton entirely too well to be interested, and anyway, when would she go out with a guy?

Friday and Saturday were the busiest nights of the week at the café. She had to be here.

What's more, she knew she wasn't any more than pretty. Lucy wasn't alone in considering herself to be the plain one in her family. Put her next to her sisters Samantha and Melissa, and she faded into the background. Disconcerting but true. *They* had regular dates.

Which was undoubtedly why her heart had bounced just because Adrian Rutledge had looked intrigued by her for one brief moment. How often did that happen?

Never?

You're pathetic, she told herself, before stealing another look out to see how he liked his lunch.

Hard to tell, when a man was chewing then swallowing.

It was two o'clock before she could escape, and then not without guilt. But Shea, her assistant cook, had shown up, and Bridget was to come at four to help set the tables for dinner. Lucy could spare a couple of hours.

Adrian had waited with apparent patience, sipping coffee and reading the weekly *Middleton Courier.*

"My mother's accident is in here," he said, closing the newspaper and folding it when Lucy walked up.

"Well, of course it is. I told you, everyone knows her. And we don't have that many accidents right here in town."

The editor had referred to her as "the kind woman known affectionately as 'the hat lady,'" which Lucy had thought was particularly tactful. She was glad he hadn't mentioned that the hat lady was homeless. From his write-up, it sounded as if she might have been a respectable senior citizen who was borrowing a Safeway shopping cart to get her groceries home, rather than an indigent whose shopping cart was the next thing *to* a home. Adrian wouldn't have to be embarrassed after reading the article in the *Courier.*

"Where do we start?" he asked.

"The library." Lucy had already decided. "I know Wendy is working this afternoon. She was really fond of your mother."

He held open the door for her. "She's the librarian?"

Lucy nodded, and after suggesting they walk since the library was only three blocks away, she said, "Yes. Wendy's from Yakima, but she married Glenn Monsey who was working for a builder over there. Our old librarian was ready to retire when Glenn decided to come home to work with his dad, who's a contractor."

"I hadn't noticed any new building."

Was he bored? Or sneering at her town? Just because she sometimes thought Middleton was dull didn't mean she'd put up with an outsider saying so. Eyeing him suspiciously, she said, "They do more over in Sequim than here in town, but we have new houses, too. Plus, they do remodeling."

He nodded, but she wasn't sure he'd even paid attention to what she said. His steps had slowed. "You have an attorney in town."

The office that had caught his attention was narrow, sandwiched between a gift-and-card shop and Middleton's only real estate office. On the window, gold letters announced in an elegant script, Elton Weatherby, Attorney-At-Law.

She waved through the window at Mr. Weatherby, who she happened to know was seventy-four years old. He and her grandfather had been in the same grade in school. He was thin and stooped, with a white shock of hair and a luxuriant mustache that actually curled up on the ends. He waved back.

"I suppose he doesn't do much but write wills," Adrian said thoughtfully.

"Why would you think that? Middleton's a normal town with all the usual lawsuits and squabbles. He does quite a bit of criminal defense, although most of it might be small potatoes by your standards."

"Tavern brawls?"

Lucy was pleased to find that she was starting once again to dislike Adrian Rutledge. His condescension annoyed her.

"We have murder and rape and domestic disturbances, just like everyone else," she said shortly, then nodded at a business on the next corner. "We'll stop at the Hair Do later and talk to Cindy."

"Your sister mentioned her. She said Cindy cut my mother's hair."

He always said *my mother* in the same, stilted way. On impulse Lucy asked, "You must have called her *Mom* when you were a kid."

Adrian glanced at her. "That was a long time ago."

"You just always sound so…uncomfortable. As if you don't want to acknowledge her."

Out of the corner of her eye she saw his jaw muscles knot. After a minute he said, "But I have, haven't I? I'm here."

Immediately ashamed, Lucy said, "You're right. I'm sorry."

They walked in silence then, Lucy nodding at passersby whom she knew. She was very conscious that everyone was noticing them, wondering where they were going and why.

It was lowering to know that nobody would speculate, even for a minute, that Lucy Peterson had snagged herself a handsome new man. If she'd been Samantha, that's exactly what they would be thinking. But she knew all too well what they thought about her. *Poor Lucy would certainly get married someday, she was such a nice young woman and a good cook, too, but of course her husband would be a local boy, not anyone truly exciting. Because* she *wasn't exciting.*

No, today they were staring because they'd heard Adrian had come to town. People were obviously dying to know why an obviously wealthy attorney's mother had been homeless. As far as Lucy knew, she was the only person he'd talked to at all about his family history, and despite her mixed feelings about him, she would keep to herself everything he'd told her. At least until he and the hat lady were gone, and there was no reason that townspeople couldn't gossip to their hearts' content.

The library was a block off the main street, built just four years back. When Lucy was growing up, the library had been on the second story of an aging granite-block municipal building, which meant it wasn't accessible to anyone who couldn't climb the stairs. The room, cold in winter and hot in the summer, had only been about six hundred square feet. Since the new building opened, the collection had tripled and the library even had a meeting room for public use. The land it stood on was donated, and every cent spent on raising the building had been donated. Middleton was proud of its library. If Adrian sneered, Lucy was prepared to turn around and head right back to the café. She wouldn't waste another second on him.

But when they walked in he actually looked mildly impressed. "Wouldn't have thought you had the population to support a library this size."

Before she could answer, Wendy spotted them from the information desk. She rose to her feet as they approached. "Lucy! I never see you on Saturdays!"

"I brought the hat lady's son to meet you. I was hoping you'd have a few minutes to talk about her. Wendy Monsey, this is Adrian Rutledge."

They shook hands, Wendy looking him over with interest, and she suggested they go to her office. The fact that she *had* an office was one of the things she appreciated most about the new library.

Wendy was about Lucy's age, beanpole tall and skinny, with curly dark hair that tended to frizz during the incessantly rainy winter. They'd become friends right away when Glenn brought her home to Middleton. Wendy had a master's degree from the University of Washington and had been working in the Yakima public library system before coming here. She was energetic, and enthusiastic, and full of ideas.

Her office wasn't very big, and she had to lift bags of books—"Donations," she explained—from one of the chairs before they could sit.

Lucy wished the limited space didn't force her to sit quite so close to Adrian. Their shoulders brushed as they faced Wendy across her desk.

"I understand you let my mother check out books even though she didn't have an address," Adrian said.

"She was probably my favorite patron," Wendy explained. "I set aside books for her, and when she brought them back we'd talk about them. Not that many people have the time or interest in doing that. I mean, half the patrons only come in here when they need a book on writing résumés, or an automobile repair manual. Or they read nothing but mysteries, or check out only gardening books, or…"

Lucy's cheeks warmed just a little. She had a couple of gardening books checked out most of the time. She especially enjoyed the ones with lots of gorgeous photographs.

"What did she read?" Adrian asked, leaning forward slightly. "I've tried to imagine how a woman who thought she was an impoverished young lady of good breeding and small fortune in Regency England coped with modern life all around her."

Lucy looked at him sharply. Had he actually *read* Jane Austen? She wouldn't have expected that.

"She had all these supposed identities, but she was still herself, too. I don't know how to explain."

Lucy agreed, "It's as if the identity of the day was only on the surface. She'd choose different hats, and her accent would change, and even her mannerisms, but…she was always the hat lady. I could talk about gardens with her no matter whether she was Queen Elizabeth or Elizabeth Taylor. Queen Elizabeth never missed a garage sale any more than Eliza Doolittle would. Something essential stayed the same."

Wendy nodded. "And she actually lived in the here and now. But only sort of. She didn't read, oh, about politics or terrorism or anything really current. I'm not even sure how much she understood local politics or the school bond issues. She liked to read fiction and poetry and biographies. Anything Arthurian, although she always said *The Once and Future King* was the best. She did love mysteries, mostly the old ones. Josephine Tey, and Dorothy Sayers's Lord Peter Wimsey series, especially after he met Harriet Vane. *Gaudy Night* and *Busman's Honeymoon.*"

They could both see his bewilderment.

"I hooked her on some modern authors, too, though. Elizabeth George—"

"That figures," he muttered.

Wendy laughed. "She probably was more willing to try the books because of the author's name. But she liked Martha Grimes and P. D. James, too. Oh, and Ellis Peters's Brother Cadfael mysteries, although I guess we can't exactly call Ellis Peters modern." She talked about how gifted his mother was at finding the tiniest of plot flaws, and how when she really loved a book she'd bring it back with passages marked. "She'd read them aloud. She did it so beautifully, as if she were on stage. I could see how much pleasure she took in language."

Adrian stirred. "She read aloud to me when I was little." His voice was strange, as though the memories weren't entirely welcome. "Even later, when I was reading myself. At first, books just a little beyond me, like *The Wind in the Willows.* Once I was eight or nine, I'd have died before I told anyone else, but she still read a chapter to me most nights. By then, it was stuff that was way beyond my reading level. Those books by Mary Renault about Theseus."

"The King Must Die," the librarian murmured.

"Yeah. I loved those. When she left—" he cleared his

throat. "We finished *The Hobbit* the night before I left to visit my grandparents. She said we'd start *The Fellowship of the Ring* when I got home."

Heart jumping into her throat, Lucy swung to face him. "She had it! Just that one! I thought it was strange, because I didn't find the other two. It's only a paperback, and the pages are yellowing, the way older paperbacks always are. But...she must have kept it."

"She'd...already bought it. I remember thinking how fat it was and wondering how long it would take us to read it. But I really liked *The Hobbit,* so I was okay with the idea."

"Did you ever read *The Lord of the Rings?*" Lucy asked softly.

"No." His voice was harsh. "Skipped the movies, too."

"She never did, either." Wendy sounded extraordinarily sad. "I suggested them once. She said no, she was waiting."

His hands tightened on the arms of the chair. Lucy saw his knuckles go white. "Waiting? Did she say for what?"

Wendy shook her head. "Her voice trailed off and she looked so bewildered and unhappy I started talking about something else as if I hadn't noticed."

They sat silent for a moment.

Lucy and Adrian left shortly thereafter. They had reached the sidewalk when he stopped suddenly. "Can you give me a minute?"

A wrought-iron bench had been placed there for library patrons waiting for a ride. He sank onto it as if his knees had given out.

"Of course." Watching him worriedly, she sat, too.

He rested his elbows on his knees and hung his head.

He'd obviously been more shaken by talking about his mother than she'd realized.

A little shocked that he was letting her see him so agitated, Lucy waited.

After a minute, Adrian sighed and straightened. "I've forgotten so much."

"Most of us put away things from our childhood."

"I'd come pretty close to putting it all away." He didn't look at her. "Dad didn't talk about her. He didn't like it when I tried. Without a sister or brother…"

"You had no one to…to help you keep her alive."

"My grandparents, of course. But after that summer I only flew up there a couple of times for shorter visits. I think Dad would have cut *Maman* and *Grandpère* off all together if they hadn't been insistent."

Her heart wrung, Lucy said, "But you do remember. You just…haven't let yourself."

"Yeah. I suppose that's it." He turned his head at last, his attempt at a smile wry and far from happy. "You're dunking me in the deep end."

"If you'd rather not—"

"No, you're right. I'm here. Later, I'll regret it if I don't talk to people who knew her. Especially if—"

His mother died without ever opening her eyes and knowing him.

"She knew she had a son," Lucy told him. "She mentioned you several times. As if you were so wound into a memory she *couldn't* forget you. And then she'd get this look on her face." She fell silent for a moment. "I thought… I assumed her little boy had died. So I never pressed her."

"You thought her grief was what derailed her."

"Um…something like that."

His eyes narrowed. "And that made you even madder, when you discovered I was alive and well."

She couldn't seem to look away from him. "I don't know," she said honestly. "Maybe."

Once again his mouth twisted and Adrian turned his head abruptly to stare across the street again. "I can't even blame you."

"I'm sorry," she whispered.

"About?"

"Misjudging you."

He met her gaze again, his face unreadable. "Are you so sure yet that you did?"

Lucy nodded, the movement jerky. "Pretty sure."

After a moment of searching her face, he said, "Thank you for that, then." He stood and held out a hand. "I know you don't have all afternoon. Shall we move on?"

Lucy stared at his hand, absurdly afraid that, if she laid hers in it, she would be sorry. Touching him might be dangerous to her peace of mind.

But of course she had no choice, unless she wanted to insult him, so she took his hand and let him pull her to her feet.

His grip was firm and warm and strong, his hand big enough to entirely engulf hers. Once she was standing, facing him, he seemed reluctant to release her. When he did, her fingers curled into a fist and she tucked her hand behind her back.

"I am running out of time," she said, trying to sound unaffected. "I was thinking, why don't I introduce you to Cindy and leave you to talk to her? And then you might go up to Safeway and ask for the manager. George did more for your mother than anyone. You haven't run into him at the hospital, have you? I know he'd be glad to talk to you."

A couple of vertical lines appeared between Adrian's dark eyebrows. "When will I see you again?"

He sounded...perturbed. As though he would *miss* her.

I'm in trouble, she thought dizzily, and knew she wasn't smart enough to keep herself out of it.

Before she could think better of it, Lucy heard herself say, "We could go to church tomorrow. Was your mother Catholic? She seemed drawn to Saint Mary's."

"She was raised in the Catholic church." His face tightened. "I have a vague memory of going to church with her sometimes when I was little. My father didn't approve."

Of course he wouldn't have, Lucy thought uncharitably. For the first time in her life, she was *glad* someone was dead.

Adrian studied her. "Do you mind going to a service at Saint Mary's?"

Lucy shook her head.

"What time?"

"Let's go to the second service at nine. That way Father Joseph might have time afterward to talk to us."

At some point they had started walking without her realizing.

When Adrian said nothing, she stole a look at him. "I have your mother's things at home. Maybe after church you can come and get them." In a rush she finished, "I can make us lunch."

"Is the café not open tomorrow?"

"No. It's closed on Sunday and Monday. For my sanity."

They'd reached the main street and had to pause while cars passed before crossing. Once there was a break, he put a hand on her back as if the protective gesture was as natural to him as breathing.

"That sounds good," he said, stopping on the sidewalk in front of the Hair Do to meet her eyes. "Thank you, Lucy Peterson. For everything."

Flustered, she argued, "It's...not so much."

"Yes. It is." He held open the door to the hair salon. "After you."

Hoping she wasn't blushing furiously, Lucy went in.

CHAPTER FIVE

ADRIAN DID NOT GO to the café for dinner. He dined on a surprisingly good filet mignon and baked potato at the Steak House, where not a soul evinced any sign of knowing who he was. He had bought a newspaper earlier in the day and not had a chance to read beyond the front page headlines; now he read while he ate, discovering that the Mariners had lost to Texas, that the Seattle city council had another ludicrous idea for replacing the Alaska Way Viaduct, and that the ferry he had ridden over on had been dry-docked for repairs and replaced temporarily with a smaller one, meaning long lines at the terminals during school spring breaks.

By the time he folded up the newspaper and paid, he couldn't remember much of what he'd read. He hadn't been concentrating. He'd been thinking about his afternoon and what the librarian, the hairdresser and the Safeway manager had told him about his mother.

He wished Lucy had gone with him to the latter two meetings. Neither Cindy nor George had relaxed with him as readily as they would have if Lucy had been there. He'd always believed he was skilled with people, but this context was different. He was an outsider. They looked at him like everyone in this damn town did, certain his mother wouldn't have been homeless if he'd done his duty as her son.

He'd buried his guilt years ago, but now it was as if everyone in Middleton were scrabbling at the dirt with their bare hands, flinging it aside to bare the coffin enclosing all his suppressed emotions. They were doing it willfully, and, God help him, he was encouraging them.

"Crap," he muttered, then grimaced when the passing waitress turned, startled. "Sorry."

"We all have days like that," she said with a comforting smile, and continued on with a tray laden with dirty dishes. The restaurant was emptying out. Apparently Middleton shut down early, even on Saturday nights.

They all had days like this? He seriously doubted it.

He went to the hospital, exchanging greetings with the same nurse that had been on last night, and went into his mother's room, where nothing had changed.

This was the first time, Adrian realized, that he'd walked in when Lucy wasn't here, talking or reading to his mother. Tonight, the chair—her chair—was empty. The only sound was the soft *beep beep* of the monitors. He wished he'd brought something to read to the woman who lay in this bed. That was pure genius on Lucy's part. It filled the silence without requiring any real effort. He had no idea what he would have read to her, though. He hadn't brought anything from home but work. Nothing in the *Times* seemed suitable, and he'd left it behind anyway.

He walked around the bed and sat in the chair. "Hi, Mom. It's Adrian. I'm back." *Yeah, brilliant.* "I had dinner at the Steak House. I'm told you ate there sometimes." More charity, but he hadn't asked for the manager to find out what about his mother had awakened the kind impulse. He felt battered enough by what the other people had told him.

"I wonder why you picked Middleton. Did it remind you of Brookfield? It sounds like people here were pretty nice to you, so I can see why you stayed. I wish I'd known where you were, though. That you'd given me a chance."

To do what? he wondered. Commit her to a mental hospital? What *would* he have done with his mother if he'd come upon her down on First Avenue in Seattle ten years ago and recognized her in the dirty, hopeless street person looking up at him from a doorway?

He had an uncomfortable feeling he would have been embarrassed. He'd have wanted to whisk her out of sight. Get her on meds and insist they be regularized until she was a normal, functioning human being.

Except that she'd never been quite normal and he'd loved her anyway. Not for the first time Adrian tried to imagine how two people as disparate as his parents had ever imagined themselves in love. Perhaps the answer was that they'd been drawn to the qualities in each other that they themselves lacked. His father had seemed solid, the very embodiment of stability and sanity, while his mother...she had been whimsical, creative and mysterious. Maybe they'd each thought they could soak up some of the other's best qualities. If so, they'd failed. It was as if the marriage had accentuated their differences; Adrian's father had become increasingly stern, while his mother had drifted further from the here and now and from her husband.

Adrian sat looking at her face, which seemed to have

more color tonight. She could have simply been asleep. Her eyelids were traced with the pale blue lines of veins beneath the skin. As he stared, her lids quivered.

Was she trying to open her eyes? He tensed, watching, scarcely breathing for fear of missing some tiny movement. None came, and gradually he relaxed. He'd seen some reflex, no more. Or perhaps she was still capable of dreaming. If so, did her unconscious brain weave the voices she heard into those dreams?

He cleared his throat. "Today I was remembering how you read to me every night. *The King Must Die* and *The Bull from the Sea.* I went to Greece a couple of years ago. Not to Crete, but to Athens and one of the other islands. Everything I saw was colored by those books. When you get better, maybe we could go together. I'd like to see Knossos."

He rambled some more, about other books they'd read, about the jokes she'd taken such childlike delight in and still did, according to Cindy. He'd gone through a phase of thinking knock-knock jokes were the funniest thing ever. His father had refused to participate in them. His mother's face would invariably brighten and she'd say happily, "Who's there?" She had made *him* feel incredibly witty.

Adrian couldn't remember the last time he'd told a joke. He laughed at the occasional off-color ones told in the locker room at his health club, but he hadn't had a good belly laugh in...God. Years. Humor had never been uncomplicated for him again, after his mother went away.

He kept wishing Lucy would walk in, while knowing she wouldn't. She'd told him that Saturday night was her busiest of the week. The café closed at ten, but she was probably busy cleaning the kitchen and closing out the cash register until midnight or later. Visiting hours would be long over. He'd felt half-trapped by her presence before, both grateful and resentful that she insisted on being here.

Now…damn it, he wanted to tell her what Cindy and George had said. He wanted her to talk about the perplexing woman who lay in the hospital bed and who, even in her mental illness, had been a chameleon, someone different to each person who knew her. He had a suspicion that if anyone had known her through and through, it was Lucy.

"She made me laugh like no one else," the middle-aged hairdresser with cheap-looking red curls had told him.

"I know she took the food I put out back for her," the balding grocer said, "but sometimes even when I saw her come down the alley I had trouble seeing her. You know? It was like she was a ghost. Not quite there. As though she *wanted* to be invisible."

Was it Lucy who'd said she was a chameleon? But why the protective coloration around the kind, portly grocer when she was so capable of letting loose peals of laughter around Cindy of the crimson curls? Was it because George was a man, and she was afraid of men?

Adrian tried to remember how his mother had related to men back when he was a child, but in those memories it seemed he and Mom were always alone. She'd gone to some parent-teacher meetings, but his elementary school teachers had all been women. His parents hadn't entertained, that he remembered. Even then he'd known Dad was ashamed of her. There had been…not fights.

Just scenes, when his father, wearing a dark suit or even a tuxedo, had left the house in the evening and his mother had looked unbearably sad when the front door shut in her face.

Had she actually been afraid of Dad? he wondered. He'd never seen his father raise his hand to her, but he'd been very good at freezing her with one look or a few scathing words. At best he wasn't a warm man, and Adrian could recall no scrap of tenderness between them. They'd had separate bedrooms, something he'd been too young then to think twice about. Likely, to Adrian's father she'd been more like a flighty, untrustworthy child than a wife, and a child who would never grow up at that.

"Were you frightened of him?" Adrian asked, his voice low in case someone walked into the room behind the concealing curtain. "Did you have any idea what he was thinking of doing to you? When I left that day, did you have any clue what was happening?"

Thinking back, he knew she'd been odd that morning; even odder than usual. A dervish of activity, anxious he hadn't forgotten anything, checking, rechecking, hovering with the quivering intensity of a hummingbird. And yet he'd seen the sheen of tears in her eyes, which had upset him and made him exclaim, "I shouldn't go! Why do I have to go without you? I want *you* to come, Mom! Why can't you?"

She didn't quite answer. His father, who had already loaded his stuff in the car, came back brimming with impatience and tore him away.

"Mom, can't you come to the airport?" Adrian had begged, but she had shaken her head frantically, tears sliding down her cheeks, as she stood on the front porch and watched his father drag him to the car and bundle him in.

"For God's sake!" his father snapped, backing out of the driveway as Adrian pressed his hands and face to the window and breathed in ragged gasps.

He shuddered now at the memory and thought, *You did know. Not everything, but something.*

Enough to fear she might never see him again.

"Did he promise you'd get better and be able to come home if you went?" Adrian asked the silent, unresponsive woman in the bed. "Did he use me somehow?"

Again her eyelids quivered. Was he upsetting her? He couldn't imagine she understood anything he was saying. Perhaps his voice, rough with long-suppressed anger, alarmed her.

He pushed back the chair and stood. "I'm sorry. I'm not very good company tonight, am I, Mom? I should have brought something to read. Maybe tomorrow I'll go back to the library." No, he realized, tomorrow was Sunday. He'd noticed it wasn't open on Sundays. Probably nothing in town would be but the churches.

"I'll just, ah, let you sleep." If that's what she was doing. He hesitated, feeling awkward. He hadn't touched her yet. He couldn't imagine kissing her cheek. Adrian wasn't much for touching, although he had liked the feel of Lucy's back. For a ridiculous instant, he'd even imagined letting his hand slide lower.

He said goodnight and left, realizing he hadn't seen Slater today. Had he been by? Did it matter? All they could do was wait, he'd said.

Adrian wasn't a patient man.

ADRIAN ALSO WASN'T a churchgoer. As he'd told Lucy, his mother had taken him to Sunday school and then services when he was really young. But either his father must have forbidden it at some point or his mother had become too uncomfortable around so many people, because they'd quit going by the time Adrian was seven years old or so.

He had no trouble finding Lucy's house, which appeared to date from the 1930s, as much of the town did. Wood-frame, modest porch, it lacked any distinguishing architectural features but had a plain, farmhouse-style charm. The lot was good-size, and most of the houses on the block were identical. Put up by the logging company that had probably once employed nearly every man in Middleton? All had large lawns that ran together with no fences in front. Hers boasted a big fruit tree in the front that was in bloom right now.

After some hesitation that morning, Adrian had worn a suit, and was glad when Lucy came out the moment his car stopped at the curb. She wore a pretty, flowery dress and pearls in her earlobes, which he could see because she'd taken a wing of hair from each side of her face and clipped it in back. When she hopped in on the passenger side and smiled at him, his body tightened. She was pretty this morning, with high cheekbones and a pixie shape to her face, a wide mouth that smiled more naturally than it pursed when she was irritated, and creamy skin that had to feel like satin to the touch. Her neck was long and slender and pale in a world where most women tanned. Her breasts and belly would be just as pale, unbisected by the lines left by a bikini. And he knew already she had long, gorgeous legs; the filmy fabric of her dress had settled, baring the shape of her thighs and hips.

They were on their way to church, and he was getting aroused by a woman wearing a dress conservative enough not to stand out in the 1950s. What was wrong with him?

"Good morning," she said. "Do you know how to find Saint Mary's?"

"Morning." Adrian put the car into gear. "It would be hard to get lost in Middleton."

In the silence that followed, he realized how rude that had sounded. Then, worse yet, he thought, *My mother was lost here.*

Her sunniness dimmed, Lucy said stiffly, "I didn't know if you'd paid any attention to the churches."

"I drove around yesterday, after I talked to George McKenzie. I looked for it and the Lutheran Church. Someone mentioned that it runs the thrift store where she…shopped." He couldn't bring himself to say "accepted charity."

"She worked there, too. Did I tell you that?"

Startled, he looked at her. "No. Worked?"

"Sorting donations, hanging up the clothes, even putting things out for display. The thrift store is run entirely by volunteers. Your mother earned what she took."

He'd been that obvious?

"Your sister said she stopped by on… Some day of the week. Tuesday," he stated. "Because they were closed on Sunday and Monday." What had Samantha said? That they let her take what she wanted? "I assumed…"

"She helped in the day care at church, too. She didn't

usually attend services, although she liked being able to hear the hymns."

"She was crazy! People trusted her with their kids?"

Her look made him feel as if he were a grease spot she'd just noticed on her dress.

"The hat lady was gentle and sweet. She was wonderful with children, especially the little ones. They'd beam at her when they saw her. And no, she wasn't alone with the children. Mothers take turn supervising the day care."

Adrian shook his head. "I don't get it."

"What don't you get? You'd better park," she added. "This is as close as we'll find."

They had to be four blocks from the redbrick church with the gilt Jesus nailed to the cross on the spire. He took her word for it, though, and pulled in to the first spot he saw that was big enough for his Mercedes. A family in front of them was getting out of their car, everyone scrubbed and in their Sunday best, the little boy's hair slicked down, the girl's in pigtails. Adrian remembered his mother ruthlessly taming his thick hair, using spit if they neared the church and his cowlick rebelled. He'd felt as uncomfortable in a suit as that poor kid did, holding his mother's hand and dragging his feet.

He and Lucy got out, too. Adrian locked the car with the remote before dropping it in his pocket and joining her on the sidewalk. A regular parade of townspeople was streaming toward the church, and even the teenagers dressed up, not a one sullen. Wasn't there a sixteen-year-old in town who sported a nose ring?

"What don't you get?" Lucy repeated.

He liked her height. She'd be perfect to dance with.

A tall man, he'd never liked looking down at the top of a woman's head. She had an easy, comfortable stride, too, when they fell into step together.

"Why she was so easily accepted," he said. "Get offended if you want, but the truth is, she was nuts. The homeless make people uneasy. Except, apparently, in Middleton."

She was silent for a moment. "Maybe," she said at last, "that's because she was our only homeless person. And also... Well, it's not true that she was easily accepted, or even that everyone was nice to her. There are people who'd cross the street so they didn't have to get too close to her. She just...well, found refuges. Places she *was* accepted and even welcome." Sadness infused Lucy's voice. "She knew there were places she wasn't."

A jolt of anger surprised him. "Like?"

She shook her head, and he realized they'd reached the crowded front steps of the church.

He let Lucy lead the way inside and choose a pew toward the back. A few curious glances turned toward them, but she only smiled and nodded at people she apparently knew.

Father Joseph in robes and surplice proved to be elderly, his hair scant and white, his face so thin Adrian wondered if he were ill. But he had that air of certainty that clergy so often had, a kind of inner peace that comforted his flock. He spoke of forgiveness of sins small and large.

Adrian suppressed a snort. Too much forgiveness would put his law firm out of business. Somehow, he didn't think there was any danger of that happening.

A choir of children in white robes sang, their voices astonishingly pure and high and beautiful. The entire congregation sat transfixed. Lucy's face shone as she listened. Adrian could easily imagine his mother as captivated. He had trouble turning his gaze to the front. He would rather have watched Lucy.

When parishioners stood to take communion, Lucy poked him with her elbow and they slipped out. Once they were in the lobby, she said, "I thought we could visit the day care until Father Joseph is free."

Sitting there watching a ritual being repeated a hundred times or more hadn't held much appeal, but neither did checking out the toddlers. Adrian had no close friends with young children, and until these past couple of days had had only rare memories of being one himself. Still, he nodded and followed her down the steps into the basement.

The room was bright, with white paint and high windows and cheerful pictures on the walls. Several cribs stood along one wall, while kids up to maybe four or five finger-painted at a long table in the middle. A baby slept in one crib, and another sat up and shook the bars of the crib, working from a grumble to a scream. There were only two adults in the room, one a teenager and the other likely a mother. She was changing a kid's diaper at a table designed and stocked for the purpose, while the teenage girl supervised the painting.

Lucy headed right for the screamer and lifted her as naturally as if she had a brood of her own. Adrian hovered in the doorway.

"My goodness!" she told the baby, a girl—no, probably a boy despite the golden curls, given the blue striped T-shirt. "Is nobody paying any attention to you at all?"

The mother laughed. "Lucy. Here, I'll trade you. Unless you want to change his diaper?"

A boy then.

"I don't mind," Lucy said, expertly laying him out on the table vacated by a little girl now being set on the carpeted floor.

"Cruising for a new church?" the mother asked.

"No, we just wanted to talk to Father Joseph. But he'll be awhile. I have to get my baby fix." She nuzzled the little boy, whose legs kicked wildly.

The woman gave Adrian an idle glance that became more interested. "Come on in," she said cordially.

"I'm, uh, fine." He eyed a couple of toddlers squealing and running straight toward him. Thank God, they veered at the last second.

Adrian continued to hover while Lucy chatted companionably with the other woman and even the teenager, helping out with an ease that told him she'd spent plenty of time with children. All those cousins once-removed? Or maybe she'd babysat her way through her teenage years.

Did she dream of having her own children? Of course she did; she obviously adored these little ones. Lucy Peterson was made to be a mother. She hadn't mentioned a boyfriend or fiancé, but then why would she? Adrian frowned, disliking the idea of her confiding in this unknown man, maybe telling him all about the hat lady and her arrogant lawyer son.

Or did he just dislike the idea of her with a man at all?

Ridiculous. He was simply avoiding thinking about his mother and her sad life. Impatient with himself, Adrian looked away from Lucy and watched the older kids finger-painting instead.

His mother had *chosen* to spend her mornings changing soggy diapers and wiping snotty noses? If she liked children so much, why didn't he have a host of brothers and sisters?

He knew the answer, of course: his father. Adrian couldn't imagine him changing a diaper or enjoying a two-year-old. And once he realized his wife was unstable, that would have been a further deterrent. Assuming he'd ever wanted children at all. Certainly he hadn't chosen to have more when he remarried.

Adrian was surprised by a peculiar emotion that was something like jealousy. The kid in him who'd lost his mom didn't like the idea of her snuggling giggling toddlers, of her laughing with them or telling the older ones knock-knock jokes. *His* knock-knock jokes. She'd loved her Sunday mornings here, but she didn't remember him.

Annoyed to feel something so irrational, he frowned. Finding out what his mother's life had been like was one thing; regressing into childhood himself was another. So his mentally ill mother had disappeared from his life when he was ten. What if she hadn't? The average thirteen-year-old boy was embarrassed by his parents anyway. Imagine how hurt she'd have been if he'd rejected her, when Mom and me ceased to be a unit and became a lonely woman and a teenage boy who didn't want to be seen with her.

Footsteps and voices and laughter on the stairs heralded the arrival of parents to pick up their youngsters. Some ignored Adrian; a few stared covertly. Lucy chatted with nearly everyone while they claimed their offspring.

Only a few were left when Father Joseph appeared, beaming. "Lucy! I knew I'd find you down here."

She laughed. "Where else? I wouldn't need to lurk

in random day-care centers if I could just persuade Samantha to get married and start a family...."

Adrian's eyes narrowed. Why did she seem to assume her sister would get married first?

"Or choose a good man and start one yourself," the good father suggested.

Lucy's gaze strayed to Adrian, waiting to one side. Immediately, color ran over her cheeks. "Um, Father Joseph, I'd like you to meet Adrian Rutledge, the hat lady's son."

"Ah." Father Joseph held out a hand, his generous smile holding no hint of the accusation Adrian had felt from nearly everyone else. "What a blessing that Lucy found you."

Adrian accepted the handshake. "And that all of you took such good care of her."

"I think those of us lucky enough to become her friends received more than we gave. Lucy told you how much she loved the children?"

Adrian nodded, that uncomfortable feeling swelling in his chest again. "Yes."

Father Joseph's smile didn't waver, but his hazel eyes seemed to read everything Adrian felt. His tone became especially gentle. "She brought joy to them, and they brought joy to her."

Adrian swallowed. "I'm glad." He was a little surprised to realize he meant it. "I understand you let her sleep here at the church sometimes."

"Yes, we have a room with a cot. Occasionally a parishioner needs a temporary refuge from troubles at home, or feels poorly during a service and must lie down. Your mother took advantage of it rarely." He shook his head sorrowfully. "She came only on the coldest or stormiest nights."

"It was good of you to offer the room."

"Does she show any improvement?" the father asked, looking from Adrian to Lucy and back. "I haven't visited since Thursday, but I pray every day for her."

Lucy shook her head. "Not yet. Unless...?" She, too, turned her gaze to Adrian.

"Not that I could see."

He waited while Father Joseph said goodbye to a family taking the golden-haired boy, then asked, "Did my mother ever talk about her past?"

"Remembering at all upset her. Once she told me she had a boy. 'He loved to watch the ferry leave the pier,' she said. I asked where she'd lived, but she couldn't or wouldn't tell me. I suggested that one day we take a drive and ride the ferry, thinking it might bring back good memories, but she looked so frightened I didn't press her."

"I worry about the years before she came here to Middleton," Adrian admitted. "I suppose it doesn't really matter, but—"

"Of course it matters. She's your mother." Father Joseph hesitated, his face creasing. "Once she told me about riding a train for days. To go home, she said, only she didn't have a ticket and they put her off. Wherever it was, it was cold and so flat the land went on forever. She couldn't remember who she should call and got confused about where she was going anyway. Some nice people bought her a ticket back to Seattle, where she'd come from. 'I am the queen,' she said, 'so I thought I ought to see the king.' I didn't know what she meant."

Throat thick, Adrian said, "The King Street Station. That's the train station in Seattle."

"Ah." Father Joseph's face cleared. "She did see signs in everything. Was she from Seattle originally?"

"Nova Scotia. But she and my father lived in Edmonds. She must have been trying to go to her parents." He imagined her, abandoned at some small train station in Saskatchewan, and felt rage at the conductor who hadn't been able to see how desperately she needed help.

He told the priest more about his mother and his regret that he had never pressed his father for answers.

Lucy stood silent as he spoke, listening, her eyes never leaving his face. The priest talked more about his mother, too, her ability to relate to every child at his or her level, to make them giggle, to heal any woe. "Most of the mothers here adored her."

"Most?"

"There are always doubters," Father Joseph said with unimpaired serenity, but Adrian had no trouble interpreting that. Some parents hadn't trusted their children to his mother. He couldn't even blame them.

Adrian realized the room was empty but for them. Voices upstairs suggested that other people were waiting to speak to Father Joseph. He thanked him and was told, "Bless you, my son."

Feeling numb, he followed Lucy upstairs and out into the sunshine.

My mother tried to go home. He imagined the devastation of her failure. Was that when she had sought the next best thing, a place that reminded her of home?

One phone call. So little, and *Maman* would have found a way to bring her home.

Two blocks from the church, he said aloud, "She did try."

"Are you going to call your grandmother then?"

He nodded. "Yeah. I'll have to persuade her not to come. She isn't well." She'd want to anyway. Adrian walled off the worry. He'd deal with it later.

After he went through his mother's pathetic cache of possessions and tried to be a halfway pleasant lunchtime companion, the least he owed Lucy.

CHAPTER SIX

IN LUCY'S GUEST bedroom, Adrian sat in an antique rocking chair, one of his mother's many hats in his hands. He didn't know what this style was called, but it looked like the ones upper-crust women wore to the Kentucky Derby. Lightweight, cream-colored and fashioned of some woven material, it had a broad, sweeping brim to shade a lady's complexion and a cluster of peach and white silk flowers sewn to the band. The silk flowers were just a little tattered, and a dirty spot marred the brim.

Something about this hat hit him. He could see her, real as day, smiling at him from beneath the shade of her hat. She was young, and happy, and beautiful, at least to him.

He turned it slowly in his hands, then flipped it over—he didn't know why. A hair clung inside, not blond like he remembered, but white. He touched it with one forefinger and had to swallow hard to suppress…he didn't know. Tears, maybe.

Why did his mother seem more alive to him here than she did breathing in that hospital bed?

With a guttural sound, he laid the hat on the bed, hung his head for a moment, then made himself open another box.

Lucy had packed his mother's possessions carefully,

the hats in plastic boxes with lids, the clothes and mis-
cellany in cardboard boxes.

This box held a few books, a plain wooden chest and
some oddities. Like a big conch shell. Why in hell would
a homeless woman want one? Yet he could imagine her
stroking its satiny pink interior or holding it up to her
ear to listen for the beat of the ocean.

A couple of the books were from the library. Adrian
guessed that Lucy had forgotten they were there. He set
them aside to be returned. His mother wouldn't be
reading them in the near future.

At the bottom was the single paperback, *The Fellowship of the Ring*. Hardly breathing, he picked it up. Lucy
was right; it looked unread, the spine unmarred, yet the
pages were yellowed with age. He started to open it to
the beginning, then hastily closed it. Stupid, maybe, but
he'd had a sort of superstition about the damn book, one
he'd never analyzed. Tolkien made him think about his
mother, ergo he didn't think about Tolkien.

But now he realized, with a grunt of surprise, that his
feelings were more complicated than that. He *couldn't*
read it without her, not without abandoning hope. Apparently he clung to more sentiment than he'd believed.

It was in the wooden chest, Lucy had told him, that
she'd found the driver's license, the photo and the
handmade Mother's Day card. When he opened the
small chest it contained a few more pictures—a couple
of school photos of him and an old black-and-white
photograph, curling at the edges, of a little girl. His
mother as a child. Blond, thin, ethereal, yet something
already sad in her face.

He didn't understand the trinkets. A thin gold ring

with a single seed pearl, nice enough she could have gotten some money for it. Had his father given it to her? Adrian fingered it. Maybe she'd had it longer than that. As pretty as she was, she'd have had boyfriends along the way. Was this a memento of one in particular, remembered with fondness?

There was other jewelry, mostly cheap, and a few items that must have held some meaning. He didn't recognize any. Or…wait. At the bottom was a shard of porcelain, waterworn but the blue-and-white glaze still visible on one side. The style was Asian.

In a flash, Adrian remembered himself walking along a beach, gazing intently at the streaks of pebbles among the miles of ocean sand. The Oregon coast? Near Kalaloch on the Washington coast? They'd vacationed at both. He was hoping for something wondrous. A sand dollar, maybe, unchipped. Or a glass float, like the man at the gift shop had talked about, or… He saw something poking from the sand that didn't belong and pounced. In his hand lay the shard.

"Mom! Mom! Look what I found!"

She hurried to him and gazed in delight at his find. "Why, I'll bet the ocean carried that all the way here from China. See the curve? It must have come from a pot or bowl. I think that's porcelain, which means it was probably valuable. How do you suppose it got broken?"

They'd speculated, bending together over the two-inch-long shard. Finally, his hand had closed tightly over it and he'd placed it ever so carefully in his pocket, determined not to lose it. It wasn't a glass float, but it had come all the way from China. That's what Mom had said, so it must be true.

"How are you doing?" Lucy asked from the doorway.

Adrian started, his hand closing around the shard of pottery just as it had then.

"Fine," he said, voice harsh, scratchy.

She hesitated. "Lunch is almost ready. But there's no hurry."

"I think I'm mostly done." His gaze swept the pitifully few boxes. "What a life."

"Did you find anything else you remembered?"

He hesitated, then opened his hand. "This."

Lucy stepped forward and peered at it with interest. "How pretty! I've seen jewelry made with antique shards of pottery like that. Where did it come from?"

"China."

"Really? Did you go?"

She looked so interested, and was so easy to talk to, he found himself telling her the story.

"I must have forgotten about it by the time I got home. Or maybe later I lost interest but it reminded her of the fun we had on that vacation. I wonder if you'd asked her, what she'd have said about it."

Lucy sat on the edge of the bed, still gazing pensively at the worthless piece of pottery in his hand. "I grew very fond of her, but she never showed me any of her treasures. I don't know why."

"Maybe because she didn't remember why she'd kept them."

She nodded slowly. "That would have bothered her terribly. Or perhaps she remembered snatches but not enough to put them into any kind of coherent narrative. That's what distressed her the most, when some bit floated through her mind but she couldn't nail it down."

"Some bit, like the fact that she had a son?"

She frowned at him. "Do you think she forgot you because she didn't love you at all?"

Adrian hated the clutch at his throat that would have made speaking difficult. He liked to be in control. He knew underlings at the firm whispered about what a cold bastard he was, and he wouldn't have argued about the characterization. But something had happened to him since he arrived at this strange little town in the middle of nowhere.

Middle. Suddenly he wanted to laugh. Now he knew how it had received its name. It was in the middle of goddamn nowhere.

Depression swept over him. "No. I know she did." He dropped the shard into the box and closed it. "Lunch sounds good."

Lucy let him get away with the change of subject and led the way to her kitchen.

He liked her house. She'd filled it with antiques, but she hadn't gone over the top like her sister had at the bed-and-breakfast. No wallpaper, but the walls were painted with color. Moss-green in the living room, a softer shade of it down the hall above cream-colored wainscotting, rust and peach in the kitchen to set off white cabinets. He guessed they were the original ones. Old glass bottles lined the kitchen windowsill, the midday sun lighting them with soft hues. Every room had potted plants, too, all luxuriant and healthy. African violets lined the sill in the dining room, where the table was set for two with quilted place mats and a jug filled with daffodils.

The house was comfortable, Adrian decided, as well as…loved. He could see Lucy in it: nothing flashy, but the decor was serene and pretty. His mother had liked brighter colors and whimsical treasures found at garage sales and art fairs, all of which had disappeared from her house shortly after she had.

"Smells good," he said, meaning it.

"I should have asked if you liked Mexican. We're having black-bean burritos. At home I like to make different food than I serve at the café."

"No soup?"

She laughed. "Well…sometimes. And I do my experimenting at home, although not usually for company. The other day, I tried a coconut-potato soup that—"

A brisk rapping on the front door brought her around. Almost without pause, it apparently opened, and a woman called, "Yoo-hoo! Are you home, Lucy?"

"Crap," she muttered.

"Lucy, dear!" another voice chimed in.

Adrian thought he heard Lucy growl.

"In the kitchen," she said, unnecessarily, for two women appeared in the doorway.

Both studied him with interest. "Oh, dear," one of them said. "Are we interrupting?"

Lucy had gotten over her flash of irritation—or maybe just hidden it—and said resignedly, "Mom, Aunt Marian, meet Adrian Rutledge. He's—"

"The hat lady's son," the taller, more buxom of the two said. "Weren't you at the café the other day?"

"Well, of course he was," the other woman said. "You know Lucy's taking care of him."

He could see the resemblance between Helen Peterson and Lucy. Her hair was short and styled, her eyes brown rather than blue, but the bone structure and shape of the face was the same. She'd remained as slim as her daughter. Today she wore a light blue skirt and short jacket over a white blouse.

He shook hands and mused that although the two were sisters they didn't look much alike. Marian was shorter, plump, darker-haired.

"We missed you at church," Helen told Lucy, studying Adrian quite frankly. "We thought we'd stop by to be sure you were all right."

"I took Adrian to the service at Saint Mary's so he could meet Father Joseph."

"Are you Catholic?" her aunt asked.

Lucy's eyes rolled.

He shook his head. "Mom was raised Catholic, though. She grew up in Nova Scotia. My grandmother is French Canadian."

"Really." Lucy's mother actually sounded interested. "She sounded so very British."

"My grandfather was."

They all looked at him and waited. Apparently he was expected to elaborate.

"Ah…*Grandpère* emigrated when he was a teenager. He let my grandmother decide on the church, but he talked about home a lot. That's what he always called England. Home." Adrian pictured his grandfather, tall and white-haired and invariably dressed in rumpled tweeds like any country squire. He smoked a pipe, too, although he chewed thoughtfully on it more often than he actually lit it. "He graduated from Cambridge with a first in English literature and was…a gentleman, I guess you'd say. Mom loved his stories. I suppose those were what she reached for, when she got confused."

"That makes sense," Lucy mused. "Elizabeth Barrett Browning, and Beth from *Little Women*... And of course she'd have loved *My Fair Lady*."

"But Elizabeth Taylor?" her mother asked.

"My grandfather admired her," Adrian said, recalling his grandmother's pique when *Grandpère* had rented several Elizabeth Taylor movies to share with his grandson. *Cleopatra* and *The Taming of the Shrew.* "Wait. Wasn't she in *Little Women,* too?"

"All the pieces go together, don't they?" Lucy observed.

Did they? As far as he was concerned, the missing years gaped horrifically, and he sensed that those pieces would never be found.

Lucy invited her mother and aunt to lunch. What else could she do? "I've made burritos," she told them.

"Beans?" Aunt Marian said. "You know they give me..." She cleared her throat. "Indigestion."

"No, no," her mother said. "Everyone's coming to the house. I have a turkey roasting. It's Sunday." A cardinal sin, apparently. "How could you forget?"

"I didn't forget, Mom!" Lucy's cheeks colored. "I just...well, didn't call you. I'm sorry."

So, she'd ditched her family for him. It should bother him, how pleased he was to know that.

Her mother and aunt left at last. When Lucy came back from seeing them out, Adrian said wryly, "I can guess what everyone in the family will be talking about this afternoon."

Lucy made a face. "I'm afraid so. I'm sorry. I should have known if I didn't let her know in advance Mom would come by to find out why I wasn't at church."

"Close family?" The idea was foreign to him.

"You have no idea," she said in a tone of loathing. Giving herself a little shake, she went to the refrigerator. "What can I get you to drink?"

As they poured drinks, he asked, "If you don't like having all your family nearby, why do you live here?"

She slipped by him into the dining room, enabling him to catch a scent he hadn't noticed outside. Lavender, maybe?

"I ask myself that at least every other day." Setting the drinks on the table, she sighed. "It just…happened."

"Happened?"

Dumb question; of all people, he knew how easily life just happened. Hell, hadn't most of his been in lockstep with his father's expectations?

Again, she whisked past him, not being obvious, but also clearly self-conscious about being too close to him. Adrian was glad, until he remembered how obvious her dislike had been earlier. Maybe he repulsed her.

When he offered belatedly to help, she handed him a bowl of salsa and a basket of chips, warm from the oven, then carried the casserole dish with the burritos to the table.

Once they'd sat, Lucy continued as if there'd been no interruption. "I came home from college thinking I'd work here for the summer, put away a little money for first and last month's rent when I moved to Seattle or Portland. Somewhere more exciting. I started cooking at the café, and then I had the chance to buy it, and…" She spread her hands.

They dished up, and he wasn't surprised to find her burritos were delicious. She admitted to making the salsa herself.

"What about you? I know your father was an attorney."

"Yeah, I think it was a given that I'd go in to law, too."

"Do you like it?"

Head cocked slightly, she asked as if she really wanted to know. Instead of the brusque, "Why else would I do it?" he might have returned to someone else, he found himself hesitating. Did he?

Adrian couldn't quite imagine doing anything else. It wasn't as if he'd been fixated on some other career, beyond the usual fancies any kid had. He remembered wanting to be an airline pilot at one point, a veterinarian at another. That dream withered, given that his father had never let him have a pet. Even earlier, he'd been determined to grow up to be a ferryboat captain. He supposed that had come from living in Edmonds, where they saw the ferry come and go all day long. One summer, he remembered begging to walk down to the beach beside the ferry dock almost every day.

"Mostly," he finally said, dishing up a second burrito and adding salsa and sour cream. "Although in law school—" He stopped.

"What?"

After a moment, he shrugged. "I thought I'd go into criminal law. Most law students go through a phase of imagining themselves saving the world, or at least some lives. I ended up wooed into corporate law."

"By money."

He studied her suspiciously, trying to decide whether she was disgusted or simply neutral.

"That's where the money is."

Lucy only nodded, applying herself to her plate.

"Do you dream of doing something else?"

She pursed her lips, as if giving serious thought to the question. "I love to cook. I've always imagined I'd end up an executive chef at a chic restaurant in Seattle or some other city. Someplace people actually appreciate variety and unique flavor combinations. Where they don't grumble because you don't have that potato soup on the menu *every* day."

Adrian grinned. "Didn't you tell me it was one of your best?"

"Yes, but that's not the point." She sounded indignant. "If you want to eat the same thing every day, you might as well stay home. If you're going to eat out, shouldn't you want to try something new?"

"Not necessarily. I have favorites at some restaurants. Don't you?"

"No, but I'm an adventurer." She went very still, a couple of creases appearing in her forehead. In a much smaller voice, Lucy said, "About food. I guess not in any other way."

She sounded sad, as though she were disappointed in herself for not living more recklessly.

Adrian sought for a way to comfort her, an unusual impulse for him, and finally settled on distraction.

"Why my mother?" he asked.

Her gaze flew to his. "What do you mean?"

"You obviously felt sorry for her. You're kind, so why not offer her a meal now and then? But you did more than that. Something about her must have drawn you."

She hesitated, and he wondered if she was reconsidering some glib answer, as he'd done earlier.

"A lot of things," Lucy said finally. "I loved it when she talked about books, and gardens, and when she told stories. I'd swear she'd *known* Bonnie Prince Charlie. Although I have to say, she made me curious enough to read a biography about him, and she was way more sympathetic to him than he deserved." She sounded indignant, as though it were his fault his mother had been such a romantic.

"At least you didn't have to dress up as him," Adrian said involuntarily.

Her eyes widened. "You did?"

He couldn't remember ever telling anyone else about the dramas he and Mom had reenacted. With a grimace, he said, "I'm afraid I wore kneesocks and an old plaid skirt of hers. I endured it only because she let me stick a steak knife in the sock. Seems as if I had a plastic sword, too."

Lucy giggled. "Oh, dear. That's a picture."

"Not a pretty one." He should have been embarrassed. Why *had* he told her? Oddly enough, her laughter let him enjoy the memory.

"Who else did you act out?"

"Oh, King Richard the First. White cross cut out of an old pillowcase, pinned on…I don't know, a red vest of Mom's, maybe?" He was thinking less about the memories than about Lucy, who listened as if she imagined herself playing out the productions with him and his mother. Her mouth, he thought irrelevantly, was very kissable when it curved like that. Almost at random, he continued, "Let's see… I was supposed to be Winston Churchill once. I read a speech into a pretend microphone. Paper towel roll, I think. My dad had a hat that looked enough like Churchill's bowler hats, I guess, to satisfy Mom. I didn't get what he—I—was saying, except that it was supposed to be noble stuff that would make his countrymen strong in wartime. Churchill wasn't anywhere near as much fun as Richard going to the Crusades."

Once again she chuckled. "History lessons wrapped in fun."

"I suppose they were. They seemed like games to me. And I'm not so sure Mom really thought she was teaching me anything. I think we acted out stories for her benefit."

"But you enjoyed them, too."

"When I was younger. By that last summer, I was starting to get embarrassed. Guys didn't dress up. I think—" He moved his shoulders uncomfortably.

Lucy finished for him. "Soon, you would have told her no."

He nodded. "I was thinking about that earlier. I felt so protective of her. But what would have happened when I got to be twelve, thirteen, and didn't want my friends to notice how weird she was?"

She looked at him with understanding. "So now you feel guilty about something that didn't happen."

"No." He scowled. "Oh, hell. Maybe. Because I was starting to have stirrings of dissatisfaction. They made me feel disloyal. Then she disappeared, and I never faced any of those decisions. Which made me wonder—" He let out a ragged breath, surprised at the force of long-ago emotions.

"You thought it might be your fault," Lucy said softly.

"Yeah. I suppose… Yeah." He rubbed a hand over his chin. "Stupid, huh?"

"Natural, don't you think? Kids are egocentric

enough to believe somewhere inside that everything happens because of them. Did you think your mom had gone away because she sensed that you were ashamed of her? Or did you think your father had gotten rid of her because he didn't think she was good for you?"

"I don't know," Adrian said slowly. "I just felt guilty. Shocked and lonely and scared, but guilty, too."

"And I suppose your father—" she named him as if he were Attila the Hun "—didn't talk to you about her or what happened."

He gave a grunt that masqueraded as a laugh. "Our sole conversation about Mom took about five minutes. After that, he froze me out if I tried to ask about her."

"What a…a creep!" She pressed her lips together. "I suppose I shouldn't say that about your father, but honestly."

"She did embarrass him. I knew even then. As far as he was concerned, a problem was solved. Years later, he looked irritated when I mentioned something that happened when we were still a family. 'Old history,' he said, like that meant it wasn't worth acknowledgement."

He could tell Lucy wanted to burst out with another condemnation of his father and barely restrained herself. Watching her struggle amused him enough that he was able to relax.

"It's okay. You won't hurt my feelings," he told her.

"Honestly!" she exclaimed again. "It's a wonder you're not in psychotherapy." She flushed. "That is, maybe you are. I don't mean there's anything wrong—"

Adrian laughed. "No. I'm not."

Maybe he should be, but the truth was that he'd learned it was easier to cut off that part of his life. Two weeks ago, if someone had asked about his mother, he'd have likely shrugged and dismissed the question. *Old history.*

God, he thought. *I've become him.*

Not a welcome realization, nor the first time he'd had it.

He couldn't pretend to know who he'd become since coming to Middleton, though. All he seemed to do was talk about his feelings, at least around Lucy. And think about 'em. Some kind of floodgate had opened, and the past was rushing through. He'd tried surfing in Hawaii once, and hated the panic that had clawed at him when he fell from the board and the waves flung him over and over until he didn't know up from down.

A kernel of that same panic knotted in his gut, and he didn't like the sensation now any better. This was idiotic. He hadn't changed because his mother had unexpectedly turned up or because he'd spent a grand total of two days in this godforsaken town. All he was doing was a research job. He'd find out what he could about his mother, then file the memories where they belonged and do what he had to for her.

End of story.

He asked Lucy…something. He couldn't have said what, but it got her talking about Middleton with a fondness she didn't seem to realize she felt. And put the conversation back where he wanted it: superficial, pleasant, unmemorable.

CHAPTER SEVEN

AFTER ADRIAN LEFT without asking when he would see her again, Lucy resolved to stay away from the hospital on Monday. The hat lady had her son now and no longer needed Lucy. If Lucy kept showing up there, it might look as if she were seeking him out.

If only she weren't attracted to him, it wouldn't have occurred to her to worry about any such thing. Since she was, she'd become ridiculously self-conscious about everything she said and did. So...the best thing was to avoid him, unless he actually came looking for her.

Having loaded the dishwasher, she added soap, set the dial to Wash and gave a firm nod. She then stood there without the slightest idea how she'd spend the rest of the afternoon, never mind all day tomorrow with the café closed.

Talk about ridiculous. Of course she had things to do. On her days off, she always had a long list of household chores and errands, never mind plans for what she'd do if only she came up with a spare hour, which she rarely did.

The trouble was, she'd gotten up extra early this morning to clean house, since she was having company, and she didn't really need groceries. Most every business in town was closed on Sunday and she had no particular errands to run anyway.

She could be lazy and read. Pour some lemonade and take it and her book outside, since the day was so nice.

But despite the early-morning housecleaning and the cooking, Lucy still felt…restless. She wanted to think over everything she'd learned about the hat lady and her son, but she wanted to be doing something while she thought.

Maybe…why, maybe she'd dig out the flower bed under the front window that she'd dreamed about for so long. She hadn't decided what to put in it yet, but digging the sod out and amending the soil would be plenty of work for one—or even two—days. Think how much fun it would be then to go to the nursery and pick out the plants.

A pang struck her, because the hat lady wouldn't be with her to help decide. But this could be…well, a sort of tribute.

No, she decided hastily, having been struck by a deeper pang, not a tribute. That sounded like a memorial, and the hat lady could wake up anytime. Thinking about her as if she were dead was just wrong.

Still, if she did recover, she'd like knowing that Lucy had finally started the garden they'd so often talked about. And this single bed beneath the window was only the beginning; there'd be more the hat lady could help with.

If her son didn't sweep her away to a nursing home in Seattle.

Adrian wouldn't do that if she *really* recovered, would he? If so, Lucy decided she'd have her for visits. The hat lady could see all her friends and favorite haunts, and they could plan the garden.

A bed on the other side of the porch, Lucy was certain about that, and ones extending to each side of the walkway. She wanted an arch covered with roses and clematis, too, right there where her concrete walk turned in from the sidewalk. She'd always wished she had boxwood hedges, too, but they took so long to grow...

Well, it's past time you start, she told herself, and quit just imagining. She couldn't even think why she *had* hesitated so long. Had she become too used to plodding along day to day, not taking time to do anything just to please herself? Or was it the other way around, that she'd been secretly afraid starting a garden was an acknowledgement that she wasn't going anywhere after all?

She found both possibilities disquieting, but refused to examine them too closely. Today, she would make a beginning.

Leaving the dishwasher running, Lucy went to her bedroom and changed into her oldest jeans and a T-shirt with a tomato-sauce stain down the front she'd never managed to get out.

The gardening gloves she found in the garage out back were stiff from disuse and the shovel was rusting. The tire on the wheelbarrow looked a little low on air, but was still rolling. None of that was going to stop her. The gloves would become pliable, and she could take some steel wool to the shovel another day. And if she really started gardening seriously, she'd want a better wheelbarrow anyway. Maybe one of those garden carts, deep and stable.

She might as well do this right. Because—why not admit it?—she wasn't likely, daydreams aside, to sell the café and embark on some adventure. Honestly, she was beginning to wonder whether she was really disappointed in herself because she hadn't overcome all obstacles to follow some inchoate dream. Maybe what actually disappointed her most was that she didn't have any big dreams. The truth was, she was pretty contented day to day, satisfied by what she *had* achieved.

Maybe, she thought ruefully, *I'm just not very exciting, if starting a garden is one of my big dreams.*

A few minutes later, she'd dragged the hose out front and had moved it a dozen times to outline the bed she saw in her mind's eye. She stretched the hose into a curve, but decided a rectangular shape suited the house better. Not until she was satisfied with the dimensions did she start to dig.

Her shovel bit into the sod and sank deep. With triumph, she lifted out the first shovelful, reached down and shook loose dirt back into the hole, then tossed grass and roots into the wheelbarrow.

Tomorrow, she thought, *I'll sneak into the hospital when I know Adrian won't be there and I'll tell the hat lady all about the beginning of my garden.*

A real garden.

She wondered if Adrian Rutledge, buttoned-down attorney, had any hobbies or dreams. Or did he deny that side of himself because it reminded him too much of his mother?

She wondered what *he* was doing with the rest of his day. And with tomorrow.

WITHIN HALF an hour of leaving Lucy's, Adrian wished he'd lingered. What was he going to do with himself? Hang around the hospital all afternoon and evening?

He did feel obligated to drive straight there and settle in at his mother's bedside for another uncomfortable, one-sided talk.

She didn't look better. If anything, her face seemed more sunken today, as if the flesh had begun the process of drying up, and he was being given a glimpse of how she'd look when she was laid in her coffin. Adrian wished desperately he could see her eyes and some spark of the mother he remembered.

"I went through your things today," he told her, because the silence was worse than hearing his own voice. "I felt bad, as if I was intruding."

It was rather like that moment in childhood, he realized, when it struck you like a lightning bolt that your parents were regular people, not just Mom and Dad. And you had no idea how other people might perceive them. Heck, you weren't sure who they actually were. So you went looking.

But you were afraid of what you'd find. He had been apprehensive. He still was. He wanted his mother to be the woman he remembered—sad sometimes, yes, confused, too, but also fun and wise and capable of true joy. He didn't want to find out she'd become angry or disgusting in some way or… He didn't know. Someone else. Someone he didn't know and never would.

The mystery of where she'd gone and who she'd become ate at him. There was a reason he had blocked her out all these years. Her mysteries left a hollow in him, too. After walling himself off all those years ago, Adrian didn't like knowing that any part of his deepest self depended on another person.

Lucy Peterson's face flickered before him then, and

he wasn't sure why. Maybe because he could imagine her shaking her head and saying, "Of course we all depend on each other!" Growing up in this small town, she'd never known a day without the interconnections of family, friends and neighbors. Maybe that's why she'd come back after college. Thinking she wanted to strike out on her own was one thing; actually wrenching herself free of the web of roots that tangled with her own was another altogether. Probably she needed those to sustain her.

Adrian shook his head, thinking he'd be strangled by those same roots and all the well-meaning people.

"The conch shell is beautiful. Could you hear the ocean in it?" He leaned forward, watching his mother's face for some shadow of memory. "That piece of china, too. I remember when I found it, you telling me the ocean must have washed it all the way from China. Now, I'd just think it was a broken piece of pottery and drop it back onto the beach. But you made me think it was magical. You were good at doing that, Mom. Making ordinary things shimmer, as if they were special." He paused. "I let myself forget the way you did that. You leaving me with Dad, I guess I started seeing things more his way. I'm sorry."

He didn't even know what he was apologizing for. Letting his father have his way? Or the fact that in his grief and anger and guilt he'd *wanted* to forget his mother, who had abandoned him?

Adrian sat silent for a minute, long enough to become aware again of the muted beeps of the monitors, to hear voices and a shushed laugh outside the door, the brisk crepe-soled footsteps of a nurse passing in the hall. But the quiet in here was overwhelming, the few sounds isolated and oddly lonely. Once again, he wished he'd brought something to read aloud.

"Lucy's going to take your books back to the library. I couldn't tell if you'd read them yet or not." He paused. "I met the librarian the other day. Maybe I already told you. She misses you. She says you're her favorite patron. Now she doesn't have anybody to talk about books with."

Was his mother's color becoming worse, too? The word *waxen* had come to him when he first saw her, but now it seemed her skin had taken on a yellow tinge as well. Had the doctor noticed? Did that mean her organs were trying to shut down?

He sat back in the chair, feeling stunned. Wasn't it strange how little prepared he was for the idea that she would die without ever waking up. When he arrived Friday, he'd mostly been in shock. The idea that this frail, white-haired woman lying in the bed was his mother hadn't seemed quite real to him. Maybe it still didn't. But the woman his mother had been before she disappeared had come alive for him again, if only in the reawakening of his memories.

Looking at the prominence of her bones and the pallor of her skin, Adrian thought, *I might not need to move her to a nursing home near me.* She might simply slip away.

There might not be any need for dutiful visits. He'd never done one single thing for his own mother. He hadn't even been the one to find her.

"God, Mom…" His voice came out broken, raw. "If only I'd known…" Without thinking, he reached for her and gripped her nearest hand hard. It was warmer than he'd expected, and smaller than he remembered.

How often had he laid his hand in hers, confident she'd return his clasp, that she *liked* holding hands with him. 'Cause Mom and him were always gonna do something.

A sound tore at his throat, shocking him.

Her eyelids twitched.

Adrian stiffened and stared. A small shudder seemed to move over her face, flaring her nostrils briefly. Behind closed lids, her eyeballs moved. Was she trying to open her eyes?

"How is she?" Ben Slater asked from beside Adrian.

He started violently, then tried to cover up by straightening and rolling his shoulders to loosen the muscles.

"I don't know. Did you see how her face was moving?" It had gone still now, as if to make him a liar. "Her eyelids were twitching and she seemed to be…I don't know, trying to frown or say something or—"

The doctor laid a hand on his shoulder. "It might just have been reflexes, you know." His voice was gentle. "A random firing of neurons."

"I was thinking her color looked worse today," Adrian said.

Dr. Slater stepped closer to the bed. "I can't say I see a change, but we'll keep monitoring her kidney function."

"You don't think she is going to wake up."

"I didn't say that. Were you talking to her when her face became mobile?"

"Yeah, but I've talked to her every time I came."

"It could be the coma is becoming lighter."

Adrian suspected he was being patronized. He could imagine the cherubic doctor patting him again and saying, *There's always hope.*

What kind of hope would they be talking about

anyway? he asked himself with a surge of impatience.
No matter what, she wouldn't be the mother he remembered, who balanced on a high wire between sanity and
a world that was only in her head. The hat lady was a
homeless woman who pushed her belongings in a stolen
shopping cart and was as crazy as the current adminis-
tration's monetary policies. If she did wake up, she'd
have to be institutionalized.

Maybe what he should be hoping was that she *didn't*
wake up, hard-hearted though that was.

For a moment, he let himself imagine his father's
reaction if he'd still been alive. He'd be impatient, disdainful, distant. You'd never know this woman had ever
meant anything to him. He'd have driven over here to
Middleton, looked to verify her identity, made the
decision immediately to move her to long-term care,
then put her from his mind except to instruct his assistant to pay the bills.

And maybe he'd have been right to be quick, ruthless
and unsentimental. Adrian had no idea what, if anything,
he was accomplishing here.

The doctor was watching him with kind eyes. "I hear
Lucy has been introducing you around town."

"She thought I could learn something about what
Mom's life has been like."

"Is it working?"

"Yeah." He pinched the bridge of his nose. "Yeah, it is."

"She was unconventional, at least by Middleton standards, but loved."

"Not by everyone."

Slater shrugged. "There are narrow-minded folks
anywhere. Got to have someone to look down on."

It sickened Adrian to know that he would have been one of those people. Oh, he'd have been polite and maybe even given her his pocket change, the way he sometimes did with the bleary-eyed bums on First Avenue in Pioneer Square. Pity didn't rule out disdain.

"It she schizophrenic?"

"It's a good possibility, from what Lucy tells me. I didn't know your mother well. The wife and I go to a different church, and me, I've dedicated myself to whacking a white ball around eighteen holes and sometimes even thirty-six at least five days a week. Our paths didn't have occasion to cross much."

"Can she be medicated?"

"If she comes out of the coma? Sure. Will she become instantly normal? Probably not. Twenty years have made her what she is." He surveyed Adrian keenly. "Try to remember that she's a good woman who has made countless friends, who's a stalwart at her church and at the thrift store. She's well-read. One of the things Lucy told me she appreciates most about your mother is that she notices beauty everywhere, instead of letting her eyes pass over it the way most of us do. Normally we see with new eyes only twice in our lives—once when we're children ourselves, and seeing everything for the first time, and then when we have our own children and see through their eyes. But your mother gave the people who cared about her the gift of seeing afresh. I think some of them like Lucy won't altogether lose it."

Adrian knew exactly what the doctor meant. His mother had never lost the ability to see with wonder.

Adrian had lost it the minute he came home to find his mother gone.

Lost it? His mouth twisted. Or thrown it away?

Or maybe he'd already been losing it, like any boy heading toward puberty. Maybe that was the gulf he'd felt opening between him and his mother: he'd started caring about other people's perceptions. Pretty soon he would have cared more about them than hers, and she would have been left all alone.

However his father had driven her away that summer, he'd only hastened the inevitable.

Dr. Slater moved past Adrian and took his patient's hand, talking pleasantly to her for a moment as if she could hear. His arm blocked Adrian's view of his mother's face.

Slater's voice sharpened. "You're right. Her face is becoming more mobile. Hmm." He stepped back from the railing. "You talk to her."

Adrian stood and reached for his mother's hand again. "Mom, it's me, Adrian. I'm still here. I'm all grown up. I don't look much like you remember me, but I'm the same person." Was he? He shook off the thought. "I can hardly wait to talk to you. Find out about your life. *Maman* has missed you so much. We could fly up there for a visit. She's kept your bedroom the same all these years. Wouldn't you like to see her?"

"Will you look at that?" the doctor murmured.

She seemed to have multiple tics. Her eyelids twitched, her mouth worked, muscles in her cheeks jerked.

"Something's definitely going on." Slater watched her with narrowed eyes. "When were you planning to move her?"

The question jolted Adrian. He should be heading back to Seattle Tuesday afternoon. He'd expected Carol would have a list of assisted living facilities for him to check out then.

Now, he couldn't even remember what his Wednesday appointments were. He hadn't opened a file on his laptop since he got here. He couldn't imagine being able to concentrate if he did.

"Ah…I hadn't gotten that far," he admitted. "I guess I was hoping for a change."

"Good. I'm going to ask that you not move her until we see whether her condition is changing."

Adrian nodded. "Fair enough."

"Thanks." Slater held out his hand and they shook. "I'm going to talk to your mom's nurses, make sure they're keeping a close eye on her. I might check back in later tonight."

"Thank you," Adrian said, his voice gruff.

"You're welcome. Your mom's somebody special." Dr. Slater nodded and left.

Lucy, Adrian thought with a surge of excitement. He should call her. She'd want to know there'd been a change. He pictured her rushing right over to sit beside him.

Then he remembered the family get-together and the fact that she'd spent all morning and the early afternoon with him for his benefit. He couldn't keep expecting her to drop everything.

And all those twitches might mean nothing at all. They might indicate—how had the doctor described it?—the random firing of neurons. Slater might have been pretending to more excitement than he felt, another metaphorical pat on the back. Did med school include classes on dealing with the patients' loved ones?

Forget it. She's responding to you. Keep talking to her.

He pulled his chair as close to the bed as he could get it and still accommodate his long legs, held his mother's hand and talked. Talked until he was hoarse. He started by telling her about himself: his first girlfriend, getting his law degree, the friends he'd lived with through grad school, the first time he'd addressed a jury in a courtroom, making partner at his firm. A couple of different nurses came and went, adjusting his mother's pillows and the height of the bed, shifting her slightly, talking cheerfully to her.

He moved on to rambling about anything and everything that entered his head: the Mariners coming close to making the World Series last October, their lousy beginning this spring, a pro bono case he'd taken on a couple of years ago, snippets from the newspaper.

A couple of times her eyeballs moved or her mouth puckered, but eventually he realized he wasn't getting any response. He'd probably worn her out. Deciding to think of her as taking a much-needed nap, he gently laid her hand back on the coverlet and said, "I'm going to go get some dinner, Mom. I'll come back for a little while this evening. You get some rest, okay?"

No answer.

Big surprise.

Adrian stood, stretched and walked out.

He was vaguely surprised to walk out of the hospital to find it was still full daylight. Barely past five o'clock. He hadn't been there as long as it felt. He guessed he'd head back to the bed-and-breakfast, maybe check e-mail, then decide what to do for dinner.

Lucy's house wasn't a quarter of a mile out of the way. He could drive by, see if her car was there. She'd want to know about his mother. He could keep it brief, undemanding.

A block from her house, Adrian saw her car in the driveway. She must have gone out at some point, because it had been moved. Half a block nearer, and he saw her sitting on the front porch steps. She'd been working out front, since the lawn was cluttered with a wheelbarrow, shovel, rake and a heap of what looked like discarded plastic bags.

Then he grinned. She'd dug out that flower bed she had talked about. By the time he pulled to the curb, he could see the newly turned earth. He guessed from the bags she'd dug in manure and who knew what else.

Lucy spotted him before he came to a stop. Alarm widened her eyes and she rose to her feet as he got out of the car.

"Adrian! Is everything okay?"

He'd seen the wince as she stood. She was filthy. Even her face was dirt-streaked. Her hair must have started in a ponytail, but it was straggling out now, a strand sticking to her forehead.

"Fine," he said. "If by that you mean Mom. I stopped by to tell you she's making some facial expressions. I thought for a minute her hand even tightened on mine. It might just be reflexes, but Dr. Slater seems hopeful."

"Really? She's been completely unresponsive. Oh, Adrian!" She glowed. "I was so afraid… Oh, my goodness."

"I thought you might like to know."

Her teeth sank briefly into her lower lip. "Of course I do!"

He nodded toward the dark, turned earth. "Appears you've had a busy afternoon."

"And I look disgusting," she said ruefully, but without the self-consciousness he might have expected if he'd caught any of his former girlfriends in a similar state. "I was just trying to work up the energy to go in and shower."

"It looks good."

"It will when I'm done. I just dug in a ton of manure and peat moss and bone meal. I was planning to go to the nursery in the morning. There's a great one in Sequim."

He rested a foot on one of the lower stairs, enjoying the play of emotions on her face.

"What do you have in mind?"

"A climbing rose, for starters." She turned to survey her creation. "It can climb up the porch railing. And maybe a clematis, too. They can twine together. Then a couple of shrubs. Maybe old roses. I've always wanted to grow some." She laughed. "I already told you that, didn't I? Oh, and perennials, and probably some annuals to fill in this year. It's going to be such fun. I'm awfully tempted to start digging on the other side of the porch, too. Because now it looks unbalanced, doesn't it?"

He had a sudden impulse. "What if I came and helped in the morning? I can't spend all day at the hospital. I don't know much about plants, but I can dig and haul the sod away."

She gazed at him as if he'd gone nuts. "Are you serious?"

"Sure." He felt oddly light. "I could sweat out all my frustrations."

A laugh escaped her. No, a giggle. "Now that you mention it, all that labor *was* therapeutic."

"Will I be depriving you?"

"Something tells me I'm going to hurt in the morning. I think I can do without too much more therapy."

Adrian grinned at her. "You don't hurt right now?"

She made a face at him. "Oh, yeah. Why do you think I was just sitting here?"

"Why don't you shower?" he suggested. "I could take you out to dinner."

"Oh, you don't have to—"

"I was thinking pizza. Unless you don't eat it unless you've hand-rolled the crust from organic, whole wheat flour and canned the tomato sauce yourself?"

"Are you making fun of me?"

"Wouldn't think of it," he assured her.

"Pizza and beer sounds really good, if you don't mind waiting. Um…do you want to come in?"

"I'll just sit out here," he said. From somewhere, he added, "Hollyhocks." At her startled glance, he shrugged in embarrassment. "I was just thinking of Mom."

"The flowers that reach for the sky," Lucy said softly.

"Yeah."

Her smile was as glorious as any rose in full bloom. "Definitely hollyhocks." She crossed the porch and opened the screen door. "I'll hurry."

"Take your time," Adrian told her, and sat on the top step, his back to the newel. Waiting, he felt better than he had all day.

CHAPTER EIGHT

ON THE WAY HOME from the nursery, Lucy cranked up the radio and in happy abandonment sang along with the top ten hits even though she couldn't carry a tune. Her trunk was tied down with a bungee cord, and her backseat was covered with newspapers and buried in a forest of greenery, some of which waved in her vision when she glanced in the rearview mirror.

She was happy. Ridiculously, gloriously, absurdly happy. She tried to tell herself it was because she'd actually accomplished something this weekend that pleased her and not spent it stripping the kitchen floor and picking up a prescription at the pharmacy and grocery shopping and hearing all the latest, trivial family gossip at her mother's on Sunday night.

But she knew she was kidding herself. She was floating on a wave of euphoria because Adrian Rutledge had stopped at her house yesterday and invited her out for pizza. And because, better yet, he was at her house right this minute, not only waiting for her, but also slaving in her yard because he apparently wanted to.

She was being an idiot. He'd be gone soon. Probably tomorrow, and if not then, within the week. He appreciated what she'd done for his mother. He was thanking her. Heck, he might even be a little bit lonely. It could be that he was thinking of her garden, as she had, as something that would be meaningful to his mother.

He was not falling madly in love with her, Lucy Peterson. The plain Peterson sister. Nobody ever had, and he was a particularly unlikely candidate to become the big exception.

But just for today, she refused to listen to reason. She'd had fun last night. For once, they hadn't talked about his mother. He'd listened with incredulous amusement to tales of *her* family instead. He'd asked about other people he had noticed around town, including several of the nurses and Jason Lee, the editor of the *Courier.*

She told him more about Elton Weatherby, the aging, courtly lawyer, and how residents of Middleton had had to drive to Sequim or Port Angeles to find an attorney until the 1950s. That was when Elton returned from law school at the University of Puget Sound and set up practice in his hometown.

Looking stunned, Adrian had paused with his beer stein halfway to his mouth and said, "He's been practicing for fifty years?"

"Most people have been doing whatever they do for close to that long when they retire," she pointed out. "Think about it. You start work as an auto mechanic right out of high school, you don't retire until you're sixty-five, and that's assuming you can afford to retire then, you'd have been working for, um—" she had to calculate "—forty-seven years."

"Good God," he'd said, and swallowed.

"Besides, Mr. Weatherby told me he loves the fact that he meets so many people and hears so many stories.

No day is the same as the one that came before, is how he put it."

"Is he planning to keep tottering into court until the day he turns up his toes?" Adrian asked.

"No, he'd like to find someone to buy the practice. Or even a young attorney to bring in to take over. He had bypass surgery last year. Mrs. Weatherby would like them to go to Arizona during the winter. Her arthritis is bad when it gets cold."

This time he shook his head. "Good lord."

Lucy had wondered from his amazement whether he actually liked his job. She'd had the impression he couldn't imagine going into his office every day for nearly fifty years. Of course, he probably wouldn't have to. Clearly, he made plenty of money. He could probably retire at fifty and…and do whatever rich people did. Sail the Caribbean. Lounge on the beach in Cabos San Lucas. Lucy wasn't quite sure. She thought she'd be bored without work.

Turning onto her street, she began to smile. Maybe she wouldn't be bored, not if she had a huge English cottage-style garden to maintain and kids and grandkids to cook for.

Just don't fool yourself they'll be Adrian Rutledge's, an inner voice warned.

Since she wasn't nearly that stupid, she didn't feel any compulsion to argue. Besides, that might not even be the life she wanted.

Adrian's Mercedes was parked at the curb. She pulled in to the driveway and stopped where they could unload most easily.

He'd accomplished an amazing amount while she

was gone. The wheelbarrow was currently piled high with sod, but he'd nearly cleared the rectangle under the dining-room window to match the bed she'd dug out yesterday. He was standing looking at it, but turned when she got out.

He was on his cell phone, she saw. She heard him say, "Yeah, I said clear the rest of the week."

Lucy unhooked the cord holding the trunk closed and pulled the first flat of perennials out.

"The Kendrick deposition?" he was saying, his gaze resting on Lucy. "Reschedule." He frowned as he listened. "Yeah, yeah, I'd forgotten what a time you had. Okay, then, have Crawford do it." Pause. "You heard me right."

Lucy set the flat on the grass and went back for another one.

Adrian covered the phone. "Don't carry anything too heavy. I'll be off in just a second." He went back to his conversation. "My mother's condition is…unstable. I don't want to leave until we know more. Crawford's capable of handling the Kendrick case."

He listened, returning short answers that made no sense to Lucy, finally ending the call. "That was Carol. My administrative assistant," he said unnecessarily. He set the phone on a porch step and went to Lucy's car, lifting one of the two climbing roses from the floor of the backseat. When he set it down on the grass, he read the label. "Zepherine Drouhin."

"It's supposed to be really fragrant. I like fragrance."

He nodded acknowledgement and passed her, going back to the car.

Buffeted by a surge of lust, Lucy stayed behind, pretending to be inspecting his work. Adrian Rutledge was sexy in an expensively cut dark suit, and in the polo shirt and khakis he'd worn yesterday. But put him in well-worn jeans, athletic shoes and a plain gray T-shirt that clung to broad shoulders and bared strong, tanned forearms, dishevel his hair, add sweat, dirt and a strong, earthy smell, and her knees went weak. Which made no sense, but she couldn't help herself.

"You went all out," he observed, returning with plant pots encircled in each of his arms.

She managed a cheeky grin. "It was the most fun I've had in years."

He returned the grin, looking years younger than he had when she met him, his teeth a flash of white in a dirty face. "Does that suggest there's something wrong with your life?"

She was tempted to ask if he was talking about sex. If so, it was overrated, in her opinion. Although... Lucy couldn't help wondering if sex with Adrian would be different. Way different.

"There are different kinds of fun," she said with dignity.

"Yeah, there are." His voice was deep. No longer smiling, he just looked at her, his expression thought-ful and...something more.

Lucy looked back. She suddenly had trouble breathing.

Of course, she lost her nerve and began to babble. "You've gotten so much done. I'm really impressed. I wasn't gone *that* long. And I'll bet you don't ache like I do. Obviously, I need to get more exercise."

The corners of his mouth twitched. "I run regularly. But I suspect I will be sore tomorrow. I can't remember the last time I used a shovel."

"So...you aren't going back to Seattle tomorrow?"

"You heard? No. Mom seemed to be reacting because I was talking to her. And Slater asked me not to move her until we can tell what's going on with her."

He couldn't have made it more clear that he *would* be moving his mother, or that he remained in Middleton only because of Dr. Slater's request.

"Yes, that makes sense," Lucy said with forced cheer. "Well, let me finish unloading the car and then I can help you."

"No, you start planting. I'm not far from done."

While she carried the last flat of perennials over, he disappeared around the house with the wheelbarrow to deposit his load in the pile she was now designating as her compost heap. Or maybe it was an eyesore, but at least it was in back by the alley, and it would compost eventually, wouldn't it?

She set the pots out the way she thought she wanted to plant, then rearranged them half a dozen times. Adrian gave advice a couple of times, then once he'd finished amending the soil, helped her lay out the shrubs and perennials she'd bought for his side of the porch, too.

His side. Who was she kidding?

But it was fun having the companionship of someone who had invested as much hard work as she had. He gave his full attention to such problems as whether the half-dozen hardy Geranium Johnson's Blue should be sprinkled amongst other perennials or clustered in artful drifts.

A few times, he would look down at one of the plants and say, in an odd tone, "Mom grew that."

He remembered the spiky Siberian irises and the tall Japanese anemones from her garden.

"And peonies," Adrian said reminiscently. "We had a whole row of them on top of a retaining wall along the street. Pink and white and red. It was really something when they were in bloom. Cars would stop in the middle of the street so the drivers could gawk."

Lucy had bought a couple of peonies, one for each side. She was pretty sure they needed some kind of staking, which made her wary of having too many.

They broke off to have sandwiches, which she put together quickly in the kitchen and they ate on the front porch steps. Lucy asked more about his early-morning visit to the hospital. Adrian had been disappointed that he'd found his mother unresponsive.

"Yesterday may have been a fluke. I'll go back this afternoon when we're done here." He glanced at her. "You probably have things to do, but if not—"

"I've been staying away so I didn't intrude," Lucy admitted. "I'd love to come. Except…I really need to shower first."

He looked ruefully down at himself. "Yeah, I'd better do that, too."

Having downed the sandwiches and the apples she'd sliced, they went back to work companionably. When they were done setting every single plant she'd bought into the ground, Adrian insisted on helping her clean up.

Then they stood on the grass and admired the two flower beds.

Looking satisfied, Adrian said, "Give 'em a month or two, and this is going to look great."

He wouldn't be here to see.

Ignoring her hollow feeling, she said, "I think I need some annuals to fill in. There's a lot of bare soil."

She frowned. "Maybe we should have put everything closer together."

"What, you don't believe they're going to get as big as the nursery says they will?"

She sighed. "I'm impatient. I want my garden bursting with flowers *now*."

"You want the equivalent of fast food?"

Lucy laughed at herself. "No, I don't. Fine, you've made your point."

"Isn't watching plants grow supposed to be half the pleasure?"

"I don't know. I've never actually gardened before, except for hanging baskets. I only imagined gardening. Which isn't quite the same."

"Ah." He was quiet for a moment. "Mom used to say something about possibilities."

Lucy couldn't help noticing how much more casually he now said *Mom* instead of *my mother,* in that stiff way he'd had. It was as if she'd become a real person again to him. Lucy was glad about that, if nothing else.

"Well." He stirred. "I'll head to the B and B and shower. Then I'll come back for you. Say, half an hour? Forty-five minutes?"

She nodded. "I'll be ready." When he started to turn away, she stopped him with a hand on his arm. "Adrian. Thank you. I wouldn't have gotten nearly as far without you."

"You know, I actually enjoyed myself today." He sounded surprised. "It felt…"

When he seemed unable to supply a word, Lucy did. "Real?"

"Real." His eyebrows pulled together as he seemed

to sample the concept. "Yeah. Most days, I write e-mails, I make phone calls, I file briefs. Nothing you can touch or look at a month later."

A tinge of sadness in his voice made her want to reassure him. "But...you must affect people's lives."

"Do I?" He shook himself. "Definitely time for that shower. I'll see you in a bit."

He strode to his car and got in so quickly, Lucy wondered if he hadn't wanted her to see that he felt even a moment of doubt about his life. But maybe it wasn't that. Maybe he was just determined to shut off any unwelcome reflection.

Lucy gazed once again at her new garden and, for a moment, saw it as it would be, in glorious bloom, not as the bare beginnings it now was. She imagined the hat lady beside her, nodding gently in approval, her new spring hat adorned with a riotous bouquet of silk flowers. In this picture, Adrian was there, too, debonair in a cream-colored linen suit, as if they'd all been to Ascot.

Then, smiling crookedly at her absurdity, she tore herself away and went inside to get cleaned up.

LUCY SEEMED CONTENT to stay with Adrian at his mother's bedside for a couple of hours. She was thrilled by every facial tic and refused to let him dismiss any new activity as random.

She scowled at him. "Dr. Slater didn't really say that."

"Yeah, actually he did. Although that was before," Adrian admitted, "he'd actually seen for himself how expressive her face is getting."

"Well, there you go then." She gave a firm nod, her

jaw jutting out as if to tell him she'd keep arguing as long as he wanted.

Of course, he didn't want. Sitting here in the hospital was different with Lucy beside him. She was able to talk to his mother so naturally, anyone listening in would assume she was getting responses of some sort. With her as an example, even he began to get the hang of it.

"You know," Lucy said suddenly, after talking about which old roses she'd bought and why, "none of these bouquets are fragrant."

"What?" Adrian stared at him.

She waved at the pot of chrysanthemums on the windowsill and the two bouquets on a bedside stand. He'd bought one himself downstairs in the gift shop, and had seen from the card that the other was from Lucy and George, the grocer. "Until your mom opens her eyes, she can't see them. But if we brought really fragrant flowers, maybe she could smell them."

What an idiot he'd been. Of course she was right. Adrian wanted to stand right that minute and go drag a florist away from his dinner table to make up a new bouquet.

"Like what?" he asked. "Roses?"

She wrinkled her nose. "Most florists' roses are hybrid teas and might as well be plastic. Oriental lilies—they have a powerful fragrance. No, I know what! Mom has an early lilac. We can cut our own bouquet." She smiled impishly at him. "We can do it tonight. I won't even ask. Mom'll never notice a few missing branches."

God, she was beautiful.

Stunned by the power of his realization, Adrian

wondered how he'd been so oblivious in the beginning. No, he knew why—he was used to hothouse flowers, showy and pampered. The women in his world visited their salon weekly for manicures and facials; they applied makeup skillfully, wore three-inch heels and shopped for clothes at Nordstrom or the downtown boutiques. Any pets were elegant purebreds, and the women's cars as expensive as they were.

His gaze moved over Lucy's face, now in profile, savoring her high, curved brow, the wing of her cheekbones, the slightly pointy chin with a hint of a cleft, the scattering of freckles on skin that had the translucence of a child's. She'd acquired a scratch across one cheek today, courtesy of Zepherine Drouhin, but she'd only laughed and wiped away beads of blood onto her shirt hem.

He wasn't sure what her prized climbing rose would look like in bloom, but she made him think of a wild rose—pale pink, perhaps, without complicated whorls, the few simple petals perfectly arranged on long, arching canes, the scent elusive and sweet.

Adrian didn't know how it had happened, when he'd only known her a few days, but he couldn't imagine driving away from Middleton without planning to see her again.

You know people. Lean on them. Find her the perfect job.

What if a restaurant like Veil or Earth & Ocean offered her a job as sous chef? That was the opportunity she'd dreamed about. Would she follow him to Seattle?

Did wild roses transplant into urban, postage-stamp-size gardens?

Why not? he thought recklessly. She longed for a life

more sophisticated than Middleton could give her. People here wouldn't change; fifty years from now, they'd still expect clam chowder on the menu every Friday. As talented as she was, she deserved better.

And he liked the idea of having her in his life, of exploring where this peculiar blend of tenderness and hunger he felt would take them.

"She squeezed my hand!" Lucy turned to him, her mouth forming a circle of delighted astonishment. "I'm sure she did!"

Adrian smiled at her, relaxing now that he'd figured out a course of action.

Find his mother a place in the best assisted-living facility in Seattle, and Lucy a job at her dream restaurant.

He didn't let himself think about the garden she'd created that weekend, or the café that bore her stamp, or the family that aroused amusement, exasperation and love in her. The family that sustained her.

Middleton wasn't that far from Seattle. She could visit. Maybe even keep the house.

And if she didn't like Seattle... His jaw tightened. Well, maybe he'd find that whatever he felt for her here evaporated in the real world.

"Show me," he said, and leaned forward to see the slender, long-fingered hand of this surprising woman wrapped around the arthritic hand of his mother.

And damned if he wouldn't have sworn the clawlike fingers tightened and clung to Lucy...who was beaming.

"You're coming back to us, aren't you? Thank goodness! We miss you so much. We're waiting, Elizabeth." Her voice had a hitch, softened. "Whenever you're ready."

"Whenever you're ready," he echoed, believing for

the first time that she would wake up, that he would have a chance to become reacquainted with the mother who had disappeared from his life so many years ago.

His heart seemed to swell in his chest, and he sat back in his chair.

What would it be like? Having her back? Discovering the history he hadn't understood as a child? Learning, perhaps, to hate his father?

Lucy would listen if he had to talk, he thought involuntarily. He could deal with anything, if she were there.

Damn it, he had to find a way.

ADRIAN INSISTED on taking Lucy to dinner again that evening, this time at the Steak House.

He seemed…different tonight, she kept thinking. Less tense, more confident, even expansive. She blossomed under the full force of his charm even as she felt wary.

It was relief, she tried to tell herself. She felt a little of that giddiness, too. It was really beginning to seem that the hat lady would come out of the coma and be herself again. And imagine how much stronger the spark of hope must be for Adrian!

On Friday, he'd discovered the mother he thought long dead was alive. He'd spent the past three days recovering his memories of her and at the same time assimilating the likelihood that she would never regain consciousness or know that he had found her. And now…now it looked like she would. Why wouldn't he feel like celebrating?

They waited until dusk to drive to her mother's street. Lucy knew it was silly to sneak in to her own parents' yard and steal lilac blossoms, but she didn't want to knock and have to introduce Adrian to her father and whatever stray aunts or cousins happened to be over, embroiling them both into an explanation of the change in the hat lady's condition.

Everything else in her life had to be shared with the family grapevine; that was the price of having their support. But she didn't want to share Adrian. And especially not what she felt for him, which she was terribly afraid was writ bright on her face to anyone who knew her well.

Like her mother, father or any stray aunts or cousins. Or, God forbid, her sister, who knew her best of all.

Anyway, Lucy could just imagine her father peering at her over his reading glasses, doubt weighting his voice. "Her cheek has a tic? And her eyes are rolling behind the lids, but she isn't opening them? And Ben says this means something?"

That was her father: the Eeyore of the Peterson clan. He always saw the dark cloud on the horizon. She loved him dearly, but she didn't think Adrian needed an introduction tonight.

She had Adrian park three houses down. The neighborhood dated from the fifties, and trees were large and leafed out with spring. Several of the neighbors had large lilac bushes in their yards, too, but none had blooms as far advanced as her mother's.

She and Adrian hurried through a pool of light cast by the streetlamp, then slowed in the dark beyond, peering past a snowball bush in full bloom.

"That's my parents' house," she whispered, indicating the brick rambler.

"You grew up there?" He spoke in a low voice, too.

Lucy nodded. "The lilac is the one by the front window."

The house blazed with lights. As they watched, a figure moved in front of the window. Samantha. Why was Samantha here? Lucy wondered indignantly, and knew the answer. Probably Mom had invited her so she could tell the family all about Adrian. By this time, they must know how much time Lucy was spending with him. She'd seen enough heads turn as cars passed her yard today while they were working.

Pull the drapes, she willed her sister, who instead turned and looked out the window. Lucy gripped Adrian's hand and held him back.

"Wait."

He nodded. She couldn't help noticing that he didn't disentangle his hand from hers.

"Okay, now," she whispered, when her sister turned and disappeared toward the kitchen.

"Is that Samantha?" Adrian murmured in her ear. "I thought she was supposed to be turning down my bedcovers and putting a chocolate on my pillow right about now."

"She's probably already done it."

She'd never asked what he thought of her much prettier sister. He hadn't talked about her beyond mentioning that Sam had told him about his mother's routine. With a pang of jealousy, Lucy speculated on whether her sister poured him a cup of tea and sat down to talk to him every night when he got back to the B and B. Sam was exceptionally easy to talk to. She'd never gone through the suspicious stage as a child that Lucy had. Mom made a point of telling people that even as a baby Samantha had grinned happily at complete strangers. She was a born hostess.

Mom invariably chuckled at that point. "My Lucy, why she glared at everyone at that age!"

Right now, Lucy quit worrying about Sam as she and Adrian hurried across the springy grass and pressed their backs against the brick wall of the house, just as her father walked across the living room. He didn't even glance toward the window. Once he'd vanished from sight, Lucy let out a breath she hadn't realized she was holding.

"Do you have the clippers?" she asked.

Adrian pressed them into her hand, nurse to her surgeon. She couldn't see very well; night had crept upon them from the dusk they'd started in. But she snipped several branches, freezing every time she saw movement inside.

By the time she backed away, it was all she could do not to giggle.

"The front door!" Adrian murmured in her ear, with an urgency that had her dropping to a crouch beside him. He took the clippers from her.

"I'd better get back, Mom." Samantha's voice came easily to their ears.

"You're so busy you can never stay," Lucy's mother complained. "If you're going to have guests seven days a week, you need to bring in some help. Bridget's looking for a job, you know."

"Lucy already hired her," Sam said. "Anyway, I can't afford help yet. Maybe by summer, if business is good."

"I know it will be." They embraced.

Samantha went to her car out on the street without ever looking toward where her sister and Adrian crouched beside the lilac. The front door remained open, spilling light onto the porch and walkway, until Sam was safely in her car and had started the engine. Then Lucy heard her father call something from another room, and her mother begin to answer. The door closed, cutting her off, and Samantha drove away.

Lucy's giggle escaped, and she clapped a hand over her mouth.

"Oh, dear. I should have knocked and told Mom I wanted to cut a bouquet. She wouldn't have minded."

"We don't want her to catch us now. God knows what she'd think."

She gave a hiccup. "Oh, no!"

"Shh!" She could tell from his voice that he wanted to laugh, too. "Come on. Let's run."

They raced across the lawn, Adrian towing Lucy, who clutched her stolen lilac branches in the other hand. Not until they'd reached the sidewalk and passed the big snowball bush that hid them from her parents' house did they stop, their laughter spilling out.

She hiccuped again, and they laughed even harder. It seemed natural to feel Adrian's arm around her, his breath against her cheek.

"You got the flowers?"

"Can't you smell them?" She held the armful up and he breathed in.

"You're a genius."

"Of course I am," she said on another bubble of laughter. Or was it a hiccup?

"More than a genius." His voice had changed, deepened. "I wouldn't be here if it weren't for you."

She went still inside the circle of his arm. "Trespassing on my parents' property?"

"In Middleton. Finding my mother." So quietly she barely heard him. "Finding you."

His hand touched her neck, slid up the column of her throat and lifted her chin. The next moment, his lips found hers.

CHAPTER NINE

WHEN LUCY'S MOUTH immediately softened and parted for his, Adrian forgot where they were. He forgot everything but her.

He crushed her to him, the scent of lilacs rising, and feasted on her mouth. She tasted of the Chardonnay she'd sipped with dinner, of the laugh she'd swallowed barely a moment ago. She was slim and taut and yielding, all at the same time.

Arousal was instant. Every sensation felt heightened: the cool night air, the pillow of her breasts pressed against his chest, the vibration in her throat, the stroke of her tongue. He gripped her hips and pulled her tighter against him even as her arm encircled his neck and she made a whimpering sound.

The blaze of the headlights of an approaching car seared Adrian's eyes through closed lids. He groaned and reluctantly lifted his head.

"Unless we want the whole town gossiping..."

"Oh, no!" she breathed, not the most flattering response she could have made. She whirled and started toward the car, not waiting to see the way his hands dropped heavily to his sides.

He hadn't locked the doors; she was already sitting

on the passenger side by the time the car passed them, headlights silhouetting her briefly, and Adrian got in behind the wheel. She sat rigidly, staring straight ahead.

He put the key in the ignition, but didn't turn it. "Did I crush the flowers?"

"The flowers…? Oh." Her head bent as she looked down at them, although he didn't know how much she could see. "No. I held them, um, to the side."

"Okay." He waited.

"Why don't we go to my house?" Lucy spoke in a rush. "I can trim them and put them in a vase. Then if you want you can drop them at the hospital tonight."

You *can drop them at the hospital*. No more *we*.

Adrian had believed himself to be reasonably skilled at the games men and women played. Now, he had absolutely no idea what to say. Hadn't they been working their way toward a kiss? Why did she seem upset?

"You won't come with me?" he asked, baffled.

"Oh, I don't think I'd better. I should never have taken so much time off this weekend. I need to work on my books this evening…." Her voice trailed off.

It might even be true. As a small-business owner, she likely did devote her days off to such tasks as accounting and ordering. But given that he guessed it was now eight o'clock, he wondered how much she'd actually get done tonight.

He nodded anyway, even if Lucy couldn't see, and started the car. "I'm sorry," he said.

"Sorry?" Her head turned sharply.

"That you can't take the time to come. Since this was your idea."

"You'll let me know if…if she responds?"

"I'll let you know." He drove several blocks. "I'm not sorry I kissed you."

"I'm...not sorry you did, either." She sounded so constrained, he couldn't tell what she felt.

"You don't seem happy."

"I just need to...well, think about it. Okay? I mean, you're here for a week. That's pretty temporary."

"Seattle isn't that far," he said mildly, although his hands had tightened on the steering wheel.

"I've had the impression you could hardly wait to see the last of Middleton. You're eager to move your mother." Her voice was even now, so reasonable it ticked him off.

"Give me a little credit," he said, anger edging every word. "I was somewhat in shock when you walked in and announced that the mother I thought was dead had been hanging around this little town for ten years. You think I should have embraced Middleton immediately?"

"You didn't have to be...to be condescending."

"What makes you think I was? You're sure it wasn't in your own mind?"

"Oh, come on. You were blown away to find out that Dr. Slater was actually competent enough to treat your mother."

Her hostility couldn't have been born this minute, Adrian realized in shock. He'd been right when he thought she didn't like him.

"Do you blame me? Small community hospitals don't have neurosurgeons."

"Did you think a small community hospital had a doctor competent to set a broken bone?"

He wrenched the wheel, pulled to the curb in front of her house and braked so abruptly, the seat belt bit into his shoulder. Adrian turned to glower at her. Light from a streetlamp let him see that she was fumbling one-handed to release her seat belt, and she looked... panicky.

No. God. On the verge of tears.

"Let me." He reached out.

"No!" She batted at his hand. "I can get it!"

He felt dense. It shouldn't have taken him so long to realize that he'd scared her. He didn't entirely understand why a kiss would have that effect, but he knew he wasn't wrong.

"Lucy..."

"What?" she snapped.

He sat very still, trying to make himself unalarming. "I really am sorry. It was..." *Impulsive* would be insulting, and not even entirely true. "I've been wanting to kiss you."

There was a moment during which she didn't move. Then, with a sigh, she sat back in the seat. "No, I'm sorry. I think I panicked. You're...a little out of my league."

He stared at her. "What in hell does that mean?"

"You're successful, rich. Hot. I live in some little town. I cook. I'm nothing special to look at." She let out another gusty sigh. "And I sound pathetic, don't I? I don't even mean it. I *like* myself. But I can't possibly be the kind of woman you usually—"

Adrian kissed her again. Roughly, passionately, and his fingers shoved into her hair so she couldn't escape. He let her go as suddenly.

"I don't see it that way." His voice was hoarse.

She gulped. He heard her.

"Oh."

"If you don't like me, say so. But don't put yourself

down. You're an extraordinary woman. What you did for my mother out of sheer kindness puts me to shame."

"That doesn't make me—"

When she stopped, he asked, "What?"

"Pretty," she whispered. Then, louder, "Sexy."

Baffled, Adrian said, "I wouldn't have kissed you if I didn't think you were both." How had she developed such low self-esteem? He tried not to think about his own original assessment of her. He'd been blind. An idiot.

After a moment she nodded. "Okay."

She sounded so damned equable, he could only repeat, "Okay what?"

"I like it that you think I'm pretty and sexy. And that you kissed me. And I'm sorry I was so…so old-maidish about it."

Good God, was she a *virgin?* Was it possible in this day and time?

Not likely in Seattle, but in Middleton…who knew? Adrian examined the idea and discovered that he didn't mind. Mild way of saying that he was getting aroused, thinking of it.

"You sure you don't want to come to the hospital with me?" he asked, when he wanted to say, *To hell with your sister's place. Can I spend the night?*

"Of course I will. I was being silly. Come on, let's put these in water." She flicked her seat belt off and opened the door with no trouble now that she'd calmed down.

He followed her into the house, watched her choose a vase from several in a kitchen cupboard, deftly trim the stems and arrange the spray of lilac blossoms. Their scent filled the kitchen as she worked, so heady he thought, *I'll never be able to smell lilacs again without thinking of Lucy. Of this moment.*

Lucy carried the bouquet to the car and let him buckle her seat belt. As they drove, with occasional streetlamps or headlights illuminating her face, Adrian asked, "Why do you think you're nothing special to look at?"

She was silent for a long time. He began to be sorry he'd asked. But at last Lucy said, "You know Samantha. And my other sister Melissa is a senior at WSU over in Pullman. They're both way prettier than I am. They got the blue eyes and blond hair. And curls! I heard people sometimes say that one or the other was the pretty Peterson girl. It was never me."

She had tried very hard to sound matter-of-fact, as if knowing what people said about the Peterson sisters didn't hurt her, not at all. But he also wondered if all this was in her head, because he couldn't see it, not when he pictured the sister he did know.

Adrian shook his head in disbelief. "Samantha's pretty in that Barbie-doll way. But you… You're classy." He felt inarticulate, rare for him, an attorney skilled at riveting the attention of juries. Maybe he was better in the court-room than in personal relationships. Usually he could tell a woman she was beautiful and that was all he had to say. But Lucy's vulnerability made it important for him to get this right. "You have gorgeous skin and great cheek-bones and a directness I hardly ever see. Maybe most of all, what you did for my mother makes you one in a million. I keep looking at you and thinking—"

He stopped, not wanting to put this into words. His longing was too unformed. She had a capacity for caring greater than anyone he'd ever known. When she loved, it would be completely. He could depend on that love.

He could trust her not to leave him.

Jolted, Adrian hardly heard Lucy ask, "Thinking what?"

That was what he believed deep inside? That no woman would love him enough to stay?

Why not? some voice inside asked. *If your own mother ditched you, how likely is it someone else will stick it out?*

He was usually the one to end relationships. The one who got bored. The one who couldn't imagine waking to that woman's face every morning for the next fifty years.

Or had he made damn sure he never cared enough to be sliced to the bone when she left him?

He pulled in to a parking spot at the hospital, set the emergency brake and turned his head to look at Lucy, who was watching him in puzzlement. Maybe, he thought, he just hadn't met the right woman.

Until now.

Sure. How did he know any such thing? It was this damn town. His head had been spinning since he got here. He shouldn't have canceled his appointments. A few days in Seattle would have given him some perspective. His mother didn't need him. Either she was going to wake up or not. He was deluding himself to think it was his voice leading her out of the fog.

Adrian also knew, looking at Lucy's anxious face, that he was glad not to be leaving Middleton tomorrow. He had close to a week during which he could spend as much time as possible with Lucy, figure out what he felt and where it was going. He had the sudden, reckless realization that he had been as happy today as he could ever remember being.

So to hell with perspective and distance. He'd grab what he could while he was here. Real life would intrude soon enough.

"I keep thinking I've never met anyone like you," he heard himself say. "And I want to figure out what makes you different."

"Hmm." She grinned at him. "You know what they say about the way to a man's heart."

"You can cook," he agreed.

"Wait'll you taste my potato soup."

"I might never want to leave Middleton."

Her smile faded; it seemed as if her eyes became more shadowed. But she said, "Hey, you never know. Shall we go see your mom?"

He agreed and they got out. Walking into the hospital, he had a strange feeling in his gut.

Never leave Middleton? That had been a joke. *Was* a joke. But something told him it was different for Lucy. She flirted with the idea of leaving Middleton, but would she really?

He found that he really wanted to know the answer to that question.

ADRIAN GLANCED uneasily around. "I know Middleton is old-fashioned, but, uh, did we just cross some space-time continuum?"

It was the following Saturday night, and Lucy had taken a break to walk him out to his car after he had dinner at the café.

Now she followed his gaze to the teenagers sashaying down the sidewalk and laughed. The girls wore poodle skirts and ponytails, and the boys had hair greased back.

"Tonight's the Spring Fling at the high school. I'm one waitress short because of it. Some of the kids must be grabbing a bite before they go on to the dance. The theme is always the Fifties. I don't actually know why."

"Wasn't there a high school in Middleton in the 1940s? What did they do then?"

"Heaven knows. Maybe you should ask Elton."

He'd had lunch the other day with Elton Weatherby, Middleton's one and only attorney. Elton had been alone at a table at her café when Adrian came in. He'd waved off Mabel, gone over to Elton and asked if he could join him. Lucy had started out of the kitchen when she first saw Adrian, and had been delighted to hear Elton say, "I hear you're a colleague, young man. By all means! By all means, pull out a chair." He'd swiveled in his chair. "Where's that girl? I've already put in an order. Now, where in tarnation has she gotten herself to? If you haven't tried the soups here, you really should."

"I've been having at least a meal a day here," Adrian had said. "Lucy's soups are damn good."

Smiling, she had gone back to the kitchen and left them to…what? Tell war stories? What *did* two attorneys discuss? Hateful judges and heroic courtroom stands? Did a corporate attorney ever make passionate pleas before a jury? She had no idea.

She hadn't actually thought to query him about what he and Elton had talked about, even though she had somehow spent quite a lot of time with Adrian that week, despite her work schedule. She'd joined him a couple of mornings for breakfast at Samantha's. Sometimes when he came in to eat at the café, she took a break and sat with him for twenty minutes or half an hour. She'd gone to the hospital with him three mornings that week.

And then there was last night, when he'd stopped by at closing and followed her car home. They had sat out on her porch glider in the dark and made out like a couple of teenagers. She'd flushed every time she thought about it today.

She had found herself singing at odd moments all week. It felt so different, having somebody waiting when she closed the restaurant, or calling at bedtime to talk about their days, or choosing his seat in the café so he could see her whenever she popped out of the kitchen. Somebody who so plainly liked to touch her. Just the way he laid a hand on the small of her back to guide her on the sidewalk made her knees weak.

What she was trying very, very hard not to think about was the fact that the week was drawing to a close. She knew he wasn't planning to leave tomorrow, but what about Monday? Wouldn't he have to go back to Seattle at some point? He hadn't said, and of course that was partly because of his mother.

It seemed that each day her coma became lighter. Ben Slater was coming by twice daily. Adrian was spending much of his time at her bedside, reading to her and talking. His voice had become gravelly from overuse.

Lucy would have loved to know what he was telling his mother. He had talked some to Lucy about the years after his mother disappeared, which sounded very sad to her. Despite his confusion and grief and buried anger, he had fallen in line with his father's expectations rather than rebelling. Having been surrounded by nosy, affectionate relatives her entire life, she couldn't imagine growing up in a household as silent as his had apparently been, and so lacking in love.

As far as she was concerned, if he retained any ability to feel love himself, it was thanks to his mom. His father must have been a very cold man.

"Oh, no! There's Uncle Will and Aunt Lynn," Lucy said now, out on the sidewalk. "You don't want to meet them, do you?"

"God, no!" Adrian said fervently, drawing her with him into the dark alcove of the doorway two businesses down from the café. Yvonne's Needle & Thread closed at five every day, which Lucy sometimes envied. Mouth close to her ear, he asked, "How many aunts and uncles do you have?"

"Oh…my mother has two sisters, both married. And Dad has a sister and a brother. That's not too bad."

He drew back to stare at her, although she doubted he could make out her face. "Not too bad? Are you kidding? That's…four aunts and four uncles. I don't even want to know how many cousins you have."

"And lots of *them* have kids, so I have cousins once removed. You're right," Lucy said agreeably. "It's horrible." She rose on tiptoe and cast her arms around Adrian's neck. "That's why I have to lurk in dark corners to get kissed."

"Hard to get by with anything in this town," he muttered, before bending his head to kiss her as requested.

Her brain immediately became as mushy as her knees. Nobody had ever kissed her the way Adrian did.

She wanted to believe it wasn't just expertise, that there was some sort of magical connection between them, but the fact that he was really good at kissing sure didn't hurt. And also, a hunger and urgency in the way he held her made her want very, very much to quit being cautious and ask him to spend the night.

But, of course, Samantha might know he hadn't returned to the bed-and-breakfast, and Sam did have a big mouth. Plus, Lucy already ached at the thought of him driving away from Middleton, even if he did promise to call. Right now, she was rather desperately holding at least some small part of herself back. If she made love with him, she was pretty sure the inevitable goodbye would be nearly unendurable.

So she backed away when his hand slid up her side and covered her breast at the same moment as he nipped her lower lip with sharp need.

"I'd better go back to work," Lucy whispered. She was trembling as the cool evening air came between them.

"I'm sorry." He sounded shaken. "I forgot—"

"It's okay." As lightly as she could manage, she said, "It was exciting, sneaking kisses out here with you."

"Can I come by tonight?" he asked with an urgency that stole what little breath she'd regained.

She didn't think she could resist him tonight. Her awareness that this week was almost over made her vulnerable.

"I'm awfully tired tonight." She sounded unconvincing to her own ears. "I really had better go back in."

He let her past, but said, "Breakfast?"

"If I don't sleep in." As if she'd be able to sleep at all, thinking about him. Ready to walk away, she couldn't.

"Why don't you come to my house instead? I'll make brunch."

"Do you *want* to cook on your day off?"

"I love to cook," she said truthfully. "It's fun just to please myself. Although I must warn you, my pastries probably aren't as good as Sam's."

His voice had relaxed, as if he'd been afraid she was rejecting him. "Her scones are amazing."

"I'll make muffins," she decided. "I froze some high bush huckleberries last year. And omelets. I can toss in anything."

"All right." He kissed her on the cheek. "I'll see you in the morning. Nine? Ten?"

"Make it ten. It's not brunch if it's too early."

He let her go, then, but she knew he was still standing by his car watching until she went back into the café.

The moment she did, her aunt called to her. "Lucy, dear! Did I miss you outside? My goodness, I haven't seen hide nor hair of you for ages."

Lucy forced a smile and went to kiss the proffered cheeks. "Uncle Will. Aunt Lynn. How are you?"

They told her, of course. Aunt Lynn was Lucy's least favorite aunt. She had a delicate stomach, she always told everyone, and invariably complained after eating Lucy's cooking that, my, she did use spices, didn't she? "I do so much better when food is milder," she would declare, as if everyone didn't know that already and avoid her offerings at family potlucks.

Lucy did like Uncle Will, however, who was a genial man who enjoyed working with his hands and who let his wife do the talking. A plumber, he had refused payment every time Lucy had had to call him. Once, he'd told her the payment in lunch that day was ample. She'd already had a particularly spicy chili simmering when her kitchen sink backed up.

"I miss food with some taste," he'd told Lucy rather wistfully, after his third bowl of chili.

She would feel sorry for Uncle Will, except that she'd seen the way he looked at his wife sometimes, as if he was still madly in love with her. Obviously, he saw a different woman than the rest of the family did.

When Lucy told them she had to get back to the kitchen, Aunt Lynn said, "You'll be at Marian's tomorrow, won't you? We missed you last Sunday. Your sister promised to bring pecan pie, and I'm bringing apple."

With only the tiniest smidgen of cinnamon, she would be sure to mention proudly.

Lucy forced a smile. "Yes, of course I'll be there. Mom put me down for potato salad."

Uncle Will's face brightened. Lucy's potato salad did not taste like his wife's.

Why, Lucy wondered as she returned to the kitchen, did she have this instinctive desire to steer Adrian away from her family? Was she afraid they'd scare him away? Or was it simply that her parents would assume it meant something if she invited a man home to meet them? She didn't know. All she was sure of was that she wanted to keep Adrian to herself. She was ashamed to realize she even hated having to share him with Sam.

If they had brunch together in the morning, would he wonder why she didn't invite him to her aunt and uncle's for Sunday dinner later? They definitely were…well, not dating, but seeing each other. Which would make it natural for her to ask him. If their positions were reversed, she was afraid her feelings would be hurt.

Of course, if she made an excuse and let him go to the hospital without her, maybe he'd never have to know…. Lucy grimaced. Uh-huh. Sure. Sam and her big mouth. It was a surprise *she* hadn't already asked him. But then, not even Sam had any idea how much time Lucy was spending with him.

But everyone in the family did know something was going on. Probably she'd make matters worse if she didn't bring him, especially after she skipped last week's Sunday dinner to spend the day with Adrian. Given that his mother had always been Lucy's "project," as the family liked to put it, they'd expect her to try to make him feel at home while he was in Middleton.

In other words…she really didn't have any choice. Not unless she wanted her nosier relatives to start speculating.

So. She'd invite him, and if he didn't make an excuse and not come, she'd be casual and friendly while they were there. Just like she always was. He wouldn't kiss her in front of her parents and other assorted family members, and once they'd had the chance to really talk to him—read, grill him—they'd lose interest. He'd merely be part of Lucy's peculiar little project.

It wouldn't occur to a one of them that her heart was going to break when Adrian left Middleton for good.

And she definitely wanted to keep it that way.

CHAPTER TEN

SUNDAY DINNER for this family was apparently a command performance. Pretty much everyone showed up, which made Lucy's decision last week to skip it so that she could have him to lunch even more noteworthy. Adrian couldn't imagine being closely related to so many people.

Fortunately, the afternoon was sunny and Lucy's aunt had set long tables out on the lawn. He didn't like to think about being crammed into the downstairs of the modest two-story house with this crowd.

Food hadn't been served yet. Since they'd arrived, Lucy had been leading Adrian from group to group, introducing him to people whose names he wouldn't remember the next time he came face-to-face with them.

The latest cluster included Lucy's mother and the same aunt who had descended on Lucy's house that time he was over. Another woman of their generation was with them.

"Have you met my aunt Lynn?" Lucy asked.

"I don't think so," he said, holding out a hand. He'd seen her, though, he realized; she was the one he and Lucy had dodged on the dark sidewalk last night.

"Lynn Rodgers," she told him. "Lucy's father is my big brother."

Aunt Marian, he seemed to recall, was Lucy's mother's sister instead.

A gaggle of screeching children raced toward them, parting at the last second to pour around them. He winced and stepped closer to Lucy.

"Are those all cousins?"

A particularly shrill giggle rent the afternoon as the kids sprang up the porch steps and vanished inside the house.

Lucy's gaze had followed them. A frown puckered her forehead. "Mostly. I don't know the redhead. Do I?"

Aunt Lynn's mouth pinched. "I believe Polly let her two both bring friends. I don't know what she was thinking. And then allowing them to behave that way."

"They're just burning off energy, Lynn," Lucy's mother said tolerantly. "They'll all be good as gold by the time we sit down to eat."

"I trust Polly will insist on *that*."

Sourpuss, Adrian thought, even though he rather hoped he wouldn't be seated anywhere near anyone younger than eighteen. If he was lucky, family tradition might put the kids at their own table.

"Goodness, Helen," Aunt Lynn continued, her gaze zeroing in on Lucy's mother. "You must be wondering why you don't have any grandchildren yet."

Her tone was a little smug, leading Adrian to realize that the unfortunate Polly was probably Lynn's daughter. Which meant some of the ill-behaved hellions were her grandchildren.

Lucy's mother laughed. "I'd just as soon my girls got married before they considered becoming parents. And, of course, my children are considerably younger than yours, Lynn."

That stung. Spots of color appeared on the sourpuss's cheeks. "Well, *mine* weren't so eager to wander all over tarnation before settling down. Assuming yours ever do."

With a quick glance at the fire in her mother's eyes, Lucy intervened. "Not fair, Aunt Lynn. Melissa's still in college, and Sam and I are stodgy members of the Middleton Chamber of Commerce. That's pretty settled."

She sniffed. "Until you start families, *I* don't consider you established. Now, if you'll excuse me, I'd best find Polly. Heaven knows what those children are up to inside. Let me apologize in advance if they damage anything, Marian."

To no one's regret, she hustled away.

"Honestly," Aunt Marian said. "How a man as nice as your Owen could have a prune-faced sister like Lynn!"

"Now, Marian," Lucy's mother said without much force.

"She's just awful," Lucy declared, earning two disapproving looks from her mother and aunt. Her chin rose. "I don't care whether you think I should say it. She's just…just…"

As she struggled to find the right word, her mother said, "What will Adrian think, Lucy? Lynn's just…" She cleared her throat. "Just…"

Marian gave a hearty bray of a laugh. "We all know what she is, and so does Adrian. Young man, you probably have a few choice relatives of your own, now don't you?"

Lucy made a quick gesture that came too late. Adrian said evenly, "Actually, my family tree is pretty sparse. Both of my parents were only children, like I am."

"What a shame," Aunt Marian exclaimed. "Not even any cousins?"

The children, he saw out of the corner of his eye, were streaming out of the house now, reinforced by half a dozen who were slightly older. He flashed on a scene from the movie version of *Lord of the Flies,* with the grimy child actors, half-naked and carrying burning torches. Was it really a shame he hadn't grown up with a passel of shrieking girl cousins, or a bullying boy cousin like the one he saw deliberately trip a smaller boy, who immediately broke into angry tears?

Lucy seemed to be watching his face somewhat anxiously. "They're really perfectly nice kids. They just get a little wild sometimes."

Marian started. "Gracious, what am I thinking? Those scalloped potatoes are going to be creamed potatoes if I don't get them out of the oven."

"Do you need help?" Lucy called to their backs as the two women hurried toward the house.

"No, no." Her mother flapped a hand as she went. "You brought your potato salad. You've done your part."

"Well," Lucy said into the little silence left in their wake, "I think you've met everyone."

God, he hoped so, Adrian thought fervently. Juries didn't intimidate him; extended families did. He'd sometimes wished he had a sibling, but one would have been ample.

He looked at Lucy, whose gaze moved from group to group as if she were doing a mental inventory. Making sure she hadn't skipped Great Aunt Bertha or second-cousin-once-removed Algernon, Adrian suspected. Despite what he feared was going through her head, he enjoyed watching her, with the sunlight picking up shimmers of gold and bronze in her hair and highlighting the freckles on her nose. He didn't recall ever considering anyone's ears pretty before, but hers seemed perfect to him, delicate whorls with lobes that each held a single, tiny diamond.

He loved her neck, too, long and slender, with baby-fine hairs at her nape. He wouldn't mind nuzzling it right now.

"Maybe we could sneak around the corner of the house for a few minutes," Adrian suggested.

Alarm flashed in her eyes. "Are you kidding? There's no privacy around here. Oh. There's Samantha." She sounded relieved as she raised her voice and waved, too. "Sam!"

Sam came, a man in tow. Evidently, he was a cousin of some sort, too, rather than an actual date. He and Adrian exchanged desultory conversation for a minute, then he wandered away.

Letting the sisters' conversation wash over him, Adrian thought longingly of that morning, when he'd actually had Lucy to himself. He'd gotten to watch her cook, which meant he'd had plenty of time to appreciate her back—her tiny waist, encircled with the apron ties, gently rounded butt encased in snug jeans and the flirtatious bob of her ponytail as she moved between mixing bowls and stove.

They had talked, too, arguing politics, sharing musical tastes, trading snippets here and there of their daily lives. An hour had passed, two hours, immensely satisfying in a way in which Adrian wasn't much accustomed. It was something like a gift exchange: here's a bit of me, to which she offered a bit of herself, upon which he gained courage and gave more. Casual, but feeling important. He wanted her, yes, with an urgency he was keeping banked to the best of his ability. But he also didn't want to ruin whatever was happening between them by pressing her too soon.

He'd never had that worry before, or this sense that they were creating something delicate and easily damaged. Adrian hoped like hell that whatever it was gained some solidity soon, both because he'd like to get her in bed and because he simply had to go back to Seattle. Carol, he knew, was increasingly perplexed by his lack of interest in ongoing cases. That morning, he'd dodged a phone call from one of the firm's partners. He wouldn't get away with hanging around Middleton for another week.

After brunch, Adrian had left Lucy with a promise to come back for her at four and gone to the hospital. It had gotten so that he had a favorite parking spot, and he knew most of the women who staffed the information desk as well as the nurses on his mother's floor. Initial suspicion had melted away in the face of his seeming devotion.

Maybe real devotion, he'd thought, sitting at his mother's bedside and watching her face twitch as some kind of impulses fired in her brain. He didn't know anymore. Did he love her? The idea of her? Would he feel an instant, heartfelt connection when/if her eyes opened? Or realize anew that this woman was a stranger?

Right now, he was in the eye of the hurricane, so to speak, over the first turbulent emotions, bemused by this odd, quiet town, separated from everything familiar in a disconcertingly thorough way given how near he was geographically to Seattle. Sooner or later, he was going to be flung back into the necessity of making decisions.

The fact that his mother was so clearly battling her way free of the coma was all that kept him in this peculiar state of suspension.

The weird thing was, he would have expected to be bored and impatient, disdainful of this backward little town and the inhabitants who seemed placidly unaware that the world was passing them by. Ten days ago, he wouldn't have been able to conceive of himself enduring Sunday dinner with fifty or so relatives of a woman he'd barely met himself.

Much less, after watching their bickering, laughter and tolerance for each other's foibles, having the passing thought that it might not be so bad to have a whole bunch of people who actually cared about you even when you screwed up, who embraced even a member nobody actually liked, because she was none-theless one of them.

He was even starting to understand why Lucy had mixed feelings about the whole family thing—wanting, on the one hand, to escape their nosiness and interference, while on the other finding it hard to pull away.

He quelled a tug of anxiety by reminding himself that Seattle wasn't so far she couldn't come home often. It was a perfect compromise. Surely she'd see that.

Aunt Marian appeared on the back porch bearing a casserole dish and called, "Time to line up!" The women ferried food out to the long serving table while the men and kids scrambled for position. Even Lucy deserted Adrian to help bring out dish after dish.

That was another thing, Adrian realized, making this town feel so backward: there were definite gender roles here that had been mostly abandoned among his friends and contemporaries. He knew couples where neither of them cooked; they ate out or brought home take-out every night. One of his occasional racquetball partners, a bank trust officer, liked to cook and did most of it in his home. Not many people he knew had children; they were too busy building careers to take time out yet, and weren't sure they ever would.

In Middleton, it appeared Lucy and Samantha were the anomalies, women too engaged in their careers to get married or have children. Of course, Lucy's career was cooking and Sam's making a home-away-from-home for people with the bed-and-breakfast. He wondered what people would have thought if the sisters had gone into law or medicine or dentistry instead. Maybe a little less tolerant, a little less certain they'd "settle down" eventually.

But then he noticed the men didn't actually get their food first; their wives edged into line with them, and a few men dished up for their women. Aunt Lynn's Will, Adrian saw, was one of those. From what Lucy had told him, that was no surprise; Will probably simply chose anything bland. But Adrian also saw the way she smiled when she took it, as though—damn it—she really loved him. Go figure.

Lucy joined Adrian in line right before he reached for a plate, and quietly steered him clear of a few dishes.

"Jeri's bean dish is really awful. Most of us take some to be nice, but you don't have to." And, "Emily loves pepper. We haven't been able to cure her of it. Unless you want to clear your sinuses…"

He didn't. There was ample food to choose from, and his plate was soon heaping.

They sat squeezed together between Samantha and the cousin whose name he couldn't remember on one side, and a wheezing grandfather and his live-in nurse on the other. Lucy's side, thank God. She cut up some of the old guy's food for him. Conversation was table-wide and lively, with rejoinders shouted from one end to the other. Adrian found himself laughing more often than he remembered in a long time, sometimes at the absurdity, sometimes at a jab of surprisingly sharp wit.

The squeezed part he didn't mind. Lucy and he kept bumping arms. Her hip was snuggled cozily against his. He could turn his head and find her smiling at him from inches away.

Several assorted children were across the table from them, but Aunt Marian was right; they'd burned off their energy and were well-behaved and even semihuman. All except one boy, not more than six or seven, who kept squirming and occasionally slipping out of sight under the table. A girl who might have been ten or eleven kept hauling him back up, sometimes while still whispering with the friend on her other side. It seemed she'd had plenty of practice.

"The doctor recommended Ritalin for Jake," Lucy told him, as if reading his mind. "But Jeri is digging in her heels, and I don't blame her. He's just a boy. He's learning to read, he's actually a whiz with numbers, and why should she drug him to make teachers happy, is her theory."

His own father wouldn't have tolerated any behavior approaching hyperactivity, Adrian couldn't help thinking. He'd have been drugged into submission.

He nodded. "I've read about the concern that drugs

like Ritalin are being overused. I had a friend like Jake, and he grew up to be perfectly normal."

Once Tony Brodzinski had started playing sports, he'd been able to use all that restless energy. He'd gone on to play baseball for a couple of major league teams and was currently pitching for the Cincinnati Reds. Adrian hadn't stayed in touch with him, but other friends had.

He told Lucy about Tony, and she said with satisfaction, "Jeri will be glad to hear about him. She can use reinforcement."

On the other hand, Adrian thought, watching the kid bat away his sister's hand, knock over his milk and accidentally poke the boy on his other side in the eye with his elbow, maybe Jake could use a little help.

But his mother appeared, mopped up the mess and soothed the younger boy, issued a stern warning then went back to her seat farther down the table. Jake managed to stay still for the next two or three whole minutes. Adrian hid a grin when he saw the boy's gaze slide sideways to be sure his sister was distracted before he slithered out of sight as quick as a snake vanishing under a rock.

"*Mo-om!*" the girl complained.

"He is a handful," Lucy said with a sigh.

Adrian had never given serious thought to having children of his own. He'd even said, when friends asked, that he didn't intend to have any. What in hell did he know about raising kids? Great example his own parents had set, the one abandoning him and the other stern, demanding and distant.

But suddenly, sitting there at the long table with Lucy

on one side, Samantha on the other, a hyperactive boy bumping into Adrian's legs to escape his sister, who had also gone under the table, Grandpa Peterson cackling at a joke Lucy had just told him, Adrian knew: he wanted children.

It was a strange and bewildering feeling, this sudden sharp need to pass on his genes, his memories, to have a child count on him. Something close to panic clutched him. This was like being on a bullet train, the landscape that might have been familiar blurring because of the speed. So much was changing, so fast. Two weeks ago, he'd been contented with work, friends, condo. Now he wanted...everything. A wife, children, love, maybe even some of the chaos of this big family.

He tried to tell himself he was having a momentary impulse that he'd get over. By the time he drove off the ferry into downtown Seattle he'd have gotten over this idiocy. Lucy, he definitely wanted; all the rest of it, no.

But the panic continued to crawl over his skin like goose bumps, and he knew, deep down, that he really had changed. Lucy had found him. Something so simple, hardly even a huge effort on her part. But because she had found him, he in turn had found her, a woman with an astonishing capacity for love and kindness, thinly veiled by wariness that she'd be hurt. And because she'd brought him here to Middleton, he'd remembered the time before his mother left, when he'd known hugs and silly jokes and a playfulness he'd later had to suppress. He'd remembered being loved, being encouraged to dream.

And now he wasn't sure the man who two weeks ago he had believed himself to be existed at all.

In desperation he thought, *I have to get away. I have to find out if something in the air here is screwing with my mind.*

"Time for dessert," Lucy told him, her smile intoxicating. "I hope you saved room. Sam's pecan pie is to die for."

"What?" her sister exclaimed indignantly from his other side. "Are you telling him my pie will kill him?"

Lucy laughed. "Only from bliss."

Still dazed, he had a slice of the famous pie and a cup of coffee, the old-fashioned kind. Middleton, he had been shocked to realize soon after his arrival, not only didn't have a Starbucks, but it had no espresso stands, either. You wanted a cup of coffee in this town, you made it yourself or you signaled for the waitress at the café or the Truck-Stop Diner outside of town. They did not call black coffee Americano in Middleton. Coffee was coffee, same as it had always been. Fortunately, he liked a plain cup of black coffee, but still. It was another sign Middleton was out of step with the world just down Highway 101.

Pretty much everyone pitched in to clean up, tossing paper plates, covering leftovers and sorting out which bowls and dishes were whose. Lucy clutched her empty bowl when they left after an exhausting round of goodbyes.

The sky was a dusky purple that would rapidly darken into nightfall. He guessed the sun was still above the horizon on the other side of the Olympic Mountains, where beachgoers could watch it sink into the ocean. Adrian wondered if Lucy could be talked into running away for a couple of days. He'd love to walk the beach at Kalaloch with her, see her eyes widen in delight when she spotted a perfect sand dollar and lifted it triumphantly from the damp sand. They could sit with their backs to a driftwood log and watch the sunset, the fiery orb seeming to melt as it met the vast arch of the Pacific Ocean.

His jaw tightened. *He* couldn't run away. He had to go back to Seattle no later than the day after tomorrow. Kalaloch with Lucy would have to be deferred until he'd persuaded her to sell the café and move to his side of the sound.

If she took a job as a sous chef at a high-end restaurant, would she be able to get away? Or would he find himself waiting for her occasional night off? Perhaps a Saturday-morning breakfast, before she left for work? Perturbed, Adrian realized how inconvenient it was that her career involved such long hours that happened not to coincide at all with his working schedule. Even if she was in Seattle, when the hell *would* they see each other?

"Thank you for coming." Seated beside him as he drove, Lucy was looking straight ahead, not at him. "I know a big family gathering isn't your idea of a good time, so it was nice of you."

"I had fun," he was surprised to hear himself say—and mean. "I'm pretty sure I ate more food today than I usually do in a week, but I think I'll survive. And, damn, it was good."

"The Martin women can all cook," she said, sounding pleased. "Now, Dad's side of the family…"

Jeri, who was so fond of pepper wasn't a Martin, he remembered. On the other hand, Aunt Marian's scalloped potatoes were darn near as good as Lucy's potato salad, and an amazing rosemary chicken with pearl onions had been Lucy's mother's dish.

"It's a wonder your father isn't fat."

She chuckled comfortably. "He can eat and eat and eat without ever putting on an extra pound. He and Mom were made for each other."

Adrian stole a glance at her smiling face. He was beginning to believe that Lucy was made for him, but he was far from sure she reciprocated the feeling. He had noticed today that she'd evaded his touch a couple of times when he had lifted a hand to lay it on the small of her back. She hadn't wanted to be claimed in any visible way in front of her family. That didn't strike him as a good sign.

They reached her house, and he braced himself for her to peck him on the cheek and claim to be so tired, she'd better not sit on the porch swing with him tonight.

He pulled into the driveway, set the emergency brake, and turned off the ignition. In the sudden silence his heartbeat quickened. He had the stricken feeling that the next few moments mattered terribly, that she was on the verge of telling him something he didn't want to hear. He turned in his seat to look at her, willing her to say, "It's such a nice night, why don't we sit outside for a while?"

Say it, he willed her. Or, "Would you like another cup of coffee before you go?"

Instead, she took a very deep breath and turned, too, so that she faced him. In the dim light, cast by a street-lamp fifty yards away, he couldn't make out her expression. But her eyes were dark, and he did see her open her mouth as if to speak, close it again, hesitate, then try again.

Her words tumbled out. "Would you like to come in?"

Say, "How about a cup of coffee?" Or, "It's such a nice night…"

He blinked. "What?"

"I know it's late and if you don't want to come in—"

"I want to," he said hastily. "Of course I do." Was she kidding? He'd go anywhere with her.

Now and forever.

God. Was he crazy? He hadn't known her long enough to be thinking things like this.

Her breath escaped in a tiny gasp. "Okay."

Wait. Why was she nervous, if this was merely a casual invitation? And she definitely *was* nervous.

"Is this just for coffee? Or…?"

"Well…" She clutched the bowl as if it were a baby she was protecting with her life. "I was thinking *or.*" She pressed her lips together. "Even though Sam will know if you're even the smallest bit late, never mind stay out all night, and then the whole family will know. Unless I plead with her." Her voice firmed. "I can do that. I'll call her in the morning. Someday she'll want a secret kept, too."

"Why am I a secret?" He had to know, even though his heart was slamming in his chest and all he wanted to do was kiss her.

"Wouldn't *you* want your sex life private from your family? Especially if there were so many of them, and they all liked to gossip?"

"Yes," Adrian admitted. "I would. The sex part. I just don't want you to feel like you have to keep *me* a secret."

He couldn't see her well enough to be sure, but he suspected she was rolling her eyes. "I took you to Sunday dinner, didn't I?"

"Yeah." Suddenly, he didn't give a damn about her family, or their gossip, or about tomorrow at all. He just wanted that giant bowl to not be between them. He unhooked his seat belt and hers. "Let's go in." His voice sounded raw to his ears. "Now."

Their car doors opened simultaneously, but he was faster. They met on her side, the bowl still between them, but who was noticing?

CHAPTER ELEVEN

LUCY'S LAST THOUGHT before he kissed her was, *Please, please, don't let me be sorry I did this once he's gone.*

Then his mouth closed over hers with such raw hunger, she quit thinking at all. Or at least not very coherently. Instead, she kissed him back.

Somehow she held on to that big serving bowl. It even made it inside, if not to the kitchen. The minute the front door closed behind them, Adrian took the bowl from her. She had no idea what he did with it. He was back, impatient and oh, so male, before she could wonder.

They shed jacket and sweatshirt right there in the entry. Then he groaned and pulled her up against him, his hands gripping her buttocks, so that she couldn't help feeling his erection. She flung her arms around his neck. Instead of kissing her immediately, though, he searched her eyes.

"I want you," he said, in an odd, rough voice. "You're sure about this?"

Lucy bit her lip and, after only the smallest of hesitations, nodded. "Just a little nervous."

"Why?"

She thought she ought to warn him. "I'm not very experienced."

He went completely still. "You're a virgin?"

Lucy shook her head. "No, I had a couple of different boyfriends in college. I was trying to live wild, you see. But…well, it was just a few times, and—" She stopped.

"And?"

"Um…not that exciting."

"Ah." He relaxed. One of his hands moved from her butt up her spine, leaving a trail of fireworks behind it. "We'll have to try to improve on that."

On a burst of nerves and enthusiasm, she blurted, "I did sort of think it would be different with you."

Momentarily his hand paused and his eyes narrowed. "So this is in the nature of an experiment?" That rough, raw quality to his voice was gone; instead he sounded carefully neutral.

She must have annoyed him, Lucy realized, but she wasn't quite sure how. It wasn't an insult to let him know that she assumed he had way more experience and skill in bed, was it?

Feeling a little indignant, she said, "If I'd wanted to experiment, I wouldn't have gone so long without… you know."

"So why me?"

"You're different," she said simply. "I've never felt like I do when you kiss me."

He smiled, all charm and something that made her heart squeeze. "Good," he murmured. "You're different, too."

Of course, she wasn't different at all, unless he meant rustic or unsophisticated. He was just being nice, which she appreciated. And he *did* want her. She couldn't be mistaken about that.

"Bedroom upstairs?" he asked.

"Yes."

"Shall we do this in style?"

"What do you mean—?" She hadn't finished, when he lifted her high and her legs closed in panic around his waist. Her sandals dropped to the floor. She squeaked and grabbed tight. "I can walk!"

"But then I'd have to set you down." With one large hand he kneaded her hip, while the other hand gripped her nape. "And you feel good like this." He captured her mouth with his.

Oh, it did feel good wrapped around him like this. Her hips rocked; he groaned and thrust his tongue into her mouth.

Somehow he did make it up the stairs with her in his arms. He'd wrench his mouth from hers and climb a couple of steps, then back her against the wall and kiss her as if he needed her taste more than he'd ever needed anything in his life.

By the time they reached her bedroom, Lucy couldn't have stood on her own two legs if her life had depended on it. She trembled, aching to have him inside her.

He laid her on the bed and followed her down, planting a knee between her thighs, still kissing her even as his hand slid under her T-shirt. He stroked her belly and closed his hand over her breast, squeezing. Her nipples had hardened and pressed against his palm. If only her bra were front-opening! When she made a sound of frustration, he growled in response and pulled her to a sitting position.

Lucy lifted her arms and let him peel off the shirt, then he unclasped her bra and tossed it aside. She'd never thought much about her breasts; after all, she only wore a B cup. But Adrian looked at her with hot gray eyes that made her feel sexy.

A little shyly, she reached out and tugged his shirt up in turn. He let her pull it off. He had a glorious chest: broad and powerful without being overmuscled, the dark hair silky under her questing hands. In her curiosity, the urgency had abated, and Adrian seemed willing to let her explore. He touched her, and she touched him. He nuzzled her breasts and suckled them in turn; she kissed his chest and licked the base of his throat where she felt his pulse hammering. Lucy loved the salty taste of his skin and did it again.

He tried to laugh, but she heard the desperation in it. He said, "Maybe the next time," which she didn't understand, and pushed her onto her back. The ache in her lower belly was back, and the feel of him unzipping her jeans was almost unbearable. He pulled her panties off with the jeans.

Lucy couldn't help herself. Her thighs pressed together and her hands went down to cover herself. Adrian laughed again, but shakily. "You're beautiful, sweetheart. Don't be shy."

"I—I can't help it," she whispered.

"Would it help if I take my pants off?"

She might be even more self-conscious, but she nodded anyway, shockingly eager to see him. Adrian pulled back from her far enough to shed his khakis and shoes. Lucy's belly cramped at the sight of him. She was sure neither of her college boyfriends had been anywhere near as large. That should have frightened her but instead was awfully exciting.

He laid down on the bed beside her, on his side facing her. "Touch me," he said, his voice guttural.

Lucy stole a glance upward at his face. His eyes still had that molten look, as if heat burned inside him. He nodded once. She put her hands on his chest again. That felt almost safe. Except that he was very warm, and his heart hammered so hard it seemed to resonate through her. And the way his muscles jumped as her hands moved downward gave her a heady sense of power.

When she finally touched him *there,* his whole body spasmed. Her exploration didn't last very long. All of a sudden he pushed her onto her back and rose above her. "Sorry, sweetheart. I can't take any more."

Somehow *he* was the one exploring now, his hands sliding up her legs, tickling the sensitive skin of her inner thighs. Her legs were splayed wantonly apart with no conscious order from her. When his fingers curled in her pubic hair, her hips rose from the bed in an agony of wanting. He parted moist flesh and stroked, with her gripping his shoulders so hard her fingernails must have been digging in.

The tension rose in her belly, coiled exquisitely tight, driven as much by the sight of the expression on his face as by his touch. "Adrian?" Her voice shook. "I want you. Not just—"

"This?" His fingers drew circles.

"Please!" she gasped.

He made a raw sound and turned away. The sound of ripping made her realize he'd come prepared. Thank goodness. During the drive, she'd thought about asking, then forgot in the enormity of the decision. *She* should have bought some condoms, but she'd have had to drive to Sequim to do it. That was the trouble with a town where everyone knew you.

He was back so quickly she didn't have time to feel anything but gratitude. He stroked her again and again, pressing, pressing… No, not with his hands, they were cupping her face as he looked into her eyes and pushed slowly forward, deeper. Her breath snagged in her throat as he filled her. The sensation was amazing, exactly what she'd needed. She lifted her hips to meet him and breathed a high, "Ooh!" that would have embarrassed her at any other moment.

Every muscle in his back was rigid with restraint. His teeth bared as he paused, buried in her. Lucy closed her eyes, savored the feeling, then rocked just enough to let him know she was ready for more.

He pulled out slowly, then thrust again a little harder, a little faster. It felt so good. No, amazing. Her fingers dug into his back. Out, in, each thrust more powerful, more urgent. His chest vibrated with a groan. Lucy whimpered.

Oh, yes. She felt like a bomb with the spark racing down the fuse toward her body. She could all but see it behind her eyelids, a flare of fire crackling, almost there, almost…

She imploded, a wave of pleasure that thundered through her like a tsunami beyond anything she'd ever felt.

He let go a second later, slamming into her, his body shuddering, a groan escaping against her cheek as he pressed his open mouth to it.

Lucy held on tight and rode the wave, high on it even as it tumbled her dizzyingly over and over.

The tsunami washed out slowly, leaving tingles and ripples in its wake. Lucy lay boneless beneath him, feeling both drained and utterly relaxed and energized all at once. A secret smile curved her mouth.

Now that was an adventure!

Adrian rolled at last, taking her along so that she sprawled atop him. When she lifted her head to look down at his face, he grinned at her. "So. Was it different?"

"Yes! Oh, yes! I had no idea." She marveled. "Was it my fault before? Or the guys' fault?"

He laughed, the skin beside his eyes crinkling, and she could see he felt a little smug. "Sex is rarely as good as that was. Rarely? Try never. What we just did takes…"

When he paused, she filled in silently. *Love. It takes love.*

"Chemistry," Adrian finished. "Something special."

Love.

As quickly as joy had swelled in her chest, it evaporated, leaving her so sad she hid her face against his neck so that he wouldn't see.

His hand stroked idly down her back, kneading here, teasing there, learning her contours.

"God, I wish I didn't have to go back to Seattle," he muttered suddenly.

Lucy bit her lip so hard she tasted blood. She had an intense inner struggle to master herself, then lifted her head. "Oh? Are you having to go back right away?"

"Tomorrow morning. I've stayed longer than I should." His hand kept moving, pressing harder, imbued it seemed with some of the same tension she now felt. "I'll be back next weekend, I promise, but I have to show my face at the firm."

"Oh. What if your mother…?"

"Wakes up? She'll do it with me or without me." He

sounded grim, either because he was convincing himself his mother didn't really need him at all, or because he hated the idea of her opening her eyes when he wasn't here to greet her.

Lucy nodded, wordless, even though she couldn't imagine being in his position and heading back to work as though the mother he'd sought for over half his life wasn't about to emerge from a coma.

Maybe, she thought doubtfully, he didn't care as much as she'd wanted to believe he did. Maybe he was fighting the fact that he did care more than he was comfortable with.

Or maybe she was being naive. After all, it wasn't reasonable for him to risk his position at the law firm and with his clients so that he could linger indefinitely in Middleton, holding his unconscious mother's hand.

Yes, that was it, she decided. Wanted to believe. He was just being...realistic.

And he did say he'd be back next weekend. So he wasn't cutting and running now that he'd gotten what he wanted from her.

She gave a nod and what she meant to be an accepting smile. He searched her face, his own suddenly taut with...she didn't know. Frustration? Desire? Even anger?

At me? Lucy wondered, before he growled something under his breath and pulled her head down so that he could kiss her with a hunger as desperate as if they hadn't just made love.

It seemed he wanted her again. She hadn't thought people did it again so soon after the first time, but her body responded with startling enthusiasm. She might be heartsick, but oh, she wanted him while she had him here, with her. And he must feel the same, because before she knew it he was swearing and fumbling for another condom, and she was completely ready.

Apparently, Lucy discovered that night, sexual satisfaction was only temporary. And people could not only make love again right away, but they could also do it three times. And, after a little sleep, a fourth time.

Sleep wasn't *nearly* as important as she'd thought it was.

LUCY PUT A brave face on it, but Adrian could tell she was shocked by his departure the next morning. He'd been warning her that he'd have to go, but she'd evidently convinced herself that he would stay at his mother's side however long it took her to wake up.

If she woke up.

His faith was eroding. Yeah, her coma had become lighter. But he'd seen no change in days now. Sure, she twitched and even seemed to flinch from bright light, but did that necessarily mean she hadn't suffered acute brain damage? Reflexes weren't the same thing as the conscious self that made a person individual. Yes, there were stories about people who'd been in comas for months or even years waking up and being themselves again, but they were the exceptions. Newsworthy. What were the chances his mother would be one of them?

Unlike him, Lucy would never give up hope. Her tenacity was one of the qualities that made her so different from anyone else he'd ever known.

That had made him fall in love with her.

She'd insisted on making breakfast. Staying to eat it prolonged the misery of the goodbye, in his opinion, but he couldn't deny her anything. She chattered, and he did his best to respond without being able, an hour later, to remember a single thing either of them had said. He was willing to bet she couldn't, either.

Behind her smile, she looked so forlorn when she walked him to the door, he felt as if someone was clawing his chest open. It hurt, kissing her one more time then walking to his car. He'd wondered briefly if he was having a heart attack.

At the inn, Samantha gave him a look he ignored. He went upstairs and packed, then came down and settled his bill. Her expression relaxed slightly when he reserved the same room for Friday and Saturday night the coming weekend, and he realized she'd been indignant on her sister's behalf.

Middleton barely showed in his rearview mirror before the forest closed around the road, and within minutes he'd arrived at Highway 101. There was the sign: Middleton, 5 miles.

Five miles, and in another universe.

A semi roared by, followed by an RV and a couple of campers. People who'd taken an extended weekend over here on the peninsula, and were now heading home. They probably never even saw the sign for Middleton, or gave a passing thought to who would live out here in the middle of nowhere and why.

How in hell, he wondered again, had his mother ended up here, of all places?

Then he turned onto the highway, and Middleton fell behind him.

FOUR DAYS LATER, it seemed as remote and unlikely as Timbuktu.

Lucy, he missed. Middleton, however, took on a hazy, unreal quality in his mind, rather like the memories he'd been dredging from the distant past that included his mother. They were actual memories, yes; but perfectly recalled? Probably not. They were colored by family tensions, by his mood, by his limited understanding, and ultimately by her disappearance. He couldn't be sure anything had happened the way he remembered it.

The first day or two in Seattle, he felt buffeted by the noise and speed of traffic and the crowds and the urgency with which people strode the sidewalks. He had some trouble concentrating, would find himself gazing out the floor-to-ceiling window in his office without really seeing the cityscape beyond the glass. He kept battling a feeling that nothing around him was real.

By Wednesday, it was Middleton he knew to be unreal. He'd felt a familiar surge of anger at the shoddy research a couple of associates had done in his absence. There was ice in his voice when he told them what he thought and sent them back to do it right. He snapped out orders for Carol to put through calls or check his schedule or find out why information wasn't right where he wanted it when he wanted it. He thought about Lucy sometimes, his chest tight, about his mother less often. Middleton itself, with its old-fashioned air, seemed as illusory as a Wild West town on the Disney lot. For all he knew, residents had engaged in an elaborate conspiracy to bamboozle the big-city attorney. Why they would have bothered, he couldn't imagine, and didn't care. He was back to figuring how quickly he could get his mother moved to an assisted-living facility here in Seattle, and Lucy into his condo and bed.

He called her twice, but both conversations were briefer than he would have liked and stilted. He said, "I miss you," and she said it, too. Otherwise, she told him that no, his mother hadn't opened her eyes yet, although she thought any day it would happen, and that he'd missed the chance to try her famous potato soup today. He was the one with almost nothing to say. She wouldn't get what he'd done all day, he told himself. *You mean she wouldn't approve,* a voice whispered. She would listen with bewilderment if he tried to explain why he was fighting tooth and nail to defend a corporation engaged in unethical practices. So he didn't try, merely said, "Doing my best," when she asked if he was catching up at work.

Friday he worked until 8:00 in the evening. Adrian would have waited to drive over until morning if it hadn't been for thoughts of Lucy. Hell, if not for Lucy he wouldn't have gone at all. He'd fallen so far behind at work, he might never catch up. The last thing he should be doing was heading out of town for the weekend.

But…he couldn't get her out of his head. The café was open and busy tonight, of course, but if he got a move on he could be waiting when she closed.

Mind made up, he packed a bag swiftly and caught a late ferry to Bainbridge. He didn't go up to the observation deck, but got out of his car and leaned on the railing, catching the sea air, hearing the gulls cry and watching the sun drop behind the Olympic Mountains, jagged and white-tipped. For the first time all week, some of the tension left his neck and shoulders, the sharp-edged impatience and drive that kept him going blunted.

The drive felt weirdly familiar this time. It seemed to go more quickly, as if his car leaped eagerly forward. His thoughts kept jumping between work and Lucy, with his mother slipping in occasionally.

Why the hell hadn't Brock returned his call? If he thought he could keep dodging... Lucy's face, dirt-smudged but shining from within as she admired her newly planted flower beds. What kind of bad luck had gotten Judge Roberta Easton assigned to the ParTex case? The damned woman drove a hybrid and was a vegan, for God's sake. What were the chances she'd rule fairly when big business clashed with the Sierra Club et al? Push her into saying something inflammatory. Yeah, that might work. Then he could demand a change of courtroom. His mother, young and pretty, laughing gaily; her face shifting, changing, aging, going still and unresponsive against the white pillow. Beep, beep, beep, life support.

He couldn't remember disliking a client as much as he did Lyle Galbreath, the young CEO of ParTex, accused of sliding around environmental regulations. Listening politely, attentively, his thoughts hidden, Adrian had wondered what it would be like to defend someone he'd known for years, someone who was scared and troubled and heartsick—or, God, actually *innocent*. Someone with a good side and maybe a bad side but also a sense of remorse, who was thinking about something besides profit.

Lucy's voice, rich and expressive, reading Elizabeth Barrett Browning. Tremulous. "I want you." She'd wanted all of him. Would she still want him once she understood that his livelihood was defending scum like Lyle Galbreath? Would she want his heart?

His headlights picked out the sign: Middleton, 5 miles. He turned, darkness closing around his car, the headlights finding only the yellow stripe down the center of the deserted highway and the trees choking it on both sides. It was suddenly like being a kid who'd opened the closet door to find a path leading into a mist-wreathed forest instead of his clothes on hangers. Last time he'd felt reluctant incredulity. This time…he hardly knew. He found himself looking ahead eagerly for the first lights. There was some of the same disorientation, but also a sense of homecoming. He knew every business on Main Street. He'd smile and nod at people coming out of the café, because he'd met them, or knew they were related to Lucy however distantly, or had been kind to his mother.

Did he have time to go to the hospital first? He glanced at his watch. Would they let him in this late? Probably. In a small-town hospital like Middleton, nobody was big on rules.

The café wouldn't close for another fifteen minutes. Lucy would be stuck there for another hour at least. Adrian made up his mind. He had time.

So instead of turning to go downtown, he continued toward the hospital. His foot lifted briefly from the gas pedal when he passed Safeway. He never went by the spot where his mother had been hit without looking, as if he might see a ghostly reincarnation of the accident. Middleton seemed like the kind of place where it might even be possible.

The information desk at the hospital was dark and

deserted. Adrian made his way upstairs, remembering his first time here. Only this was different, of course. The nurse at the station looked up and beamed at the sight of him. "Mr. Rutledge! Your mother's been so restless today. I know she'll be glad you're back."

"Do you mind if I go in for a minute?" he asked. "I know it's past visiting hours—"

"Don't be silly," she said comfortably. "Take your time. She doesn't have a roommate you'd be disturbing. I haven't turned out her light yet."

"Thanks."

When he circled the drawn curtain and went to his mother's bedside, he expected her to be sleeping, as the entire hospital seemed to be around them. Instead, to his shock, he found her head turned on the pillow so that she could scowl fiercely at the empty chair. Her mouth worked, as though she desperately wanted to say something.

"Mom?" He reached out and took her hand. "Mom, it's Adrian. Are you all right?"

Stupid question. What did he expect? *Yes, dear, of course I am?*

But she gripped his hand. This time, it couldn't be in his imagination. Her fingers bit into his and her head rolled frantically on the pillow. Restless, the nurse had said. More as if she were just below the surface, fighting her way up.

"Hey. It'll come," he said. "Don't worry."

He kept murmuring nonsense, she kept twitching spasmodically and holding on to him so hard, he was afraid he'd have to all but pry her fingers from his when it came time to leave. Eventually she subsided, though, and he thought she might even be asleep by the time he slipped out. He turned off the light as he went, and told the nurse, "She seems to have settled down."

"Oh, thank goodness. I'll bet she knew you were there."

He felt a pang. She had responded to him. By the time he walked out of the hospital into the night air, however, he'd reminded himself that his mother was unlikely to have the slightest idea who he was if she did wake up. Maybe having anyone at all there holding her hand and talking to her would have calmed her.

With all the businesses closed, he was able to park right in front of the café. The front door was locked, but Mabel hurried to open it when he knocked.

"Adrian, I didn't know you were coming back today."

"I wasn't sure I could make it." He nodded toward the kitchen. "Lucy in back?"

She smiled. "I'm done out here. Tell her goodnight."

"Will do."

Surprising him, she reached out and gave his hand a squeeze. "I'm glad you came." Then she hurried out, leaving him staring after her. Did everyone in town assume he'd ditched Lucy and his mother both for the bright lights of the city?

Hadn't he come close?

"Mabel?" Lucy's voice came from the kitchen. "Is someone here?"

"Mabel says goodnight." Adrian walked toward the back.

She appeared in the doorway. "Adrian?" Her face lit. "It *is* you!"

She hadn't thought he would show up tonight, either, he realized. He'd have been ticked at her lack of faith, if guilt hadn't niggled at him for the reluctance he'd felt all day. Part of him *hadn't* wanted to ever return to Middleton. He'd been afraid....

Afraid? Of what? Adrian asked himself in shock, but didn't let himself pursue an answer he wasn't sure he had.

"Yeah," he said roughly. "It's me."

He took a couple of long strides; she flung herself at him. His arms closed around her compulsively, hers around him as tightly. His heart cramped, his eyes burned, and he thought, *Am I afraid of this?*

But he had a bad feeling it wasn't that simple.

CHAPTER TWELVE

LUCY LIFTED her head at last. "Have you been to the hospital yet?"

"Yeah." Adrian slowly, reluctantly, loosened his hold on her. "The nurse said Mom was restless. But it was more than that. It seemed as if...I don't know, as if she's fighting something I can't see."

Lucy nodded. "I almost called you this morning. I started to wonder if she can hear us now but can't quite respond. Think how frustrating that would be."

He shuddered, hating to think about her trapped, unable to scream, unable to let anyone know she was *there*. Yeah, *frustrating* was one word for it. "You should have called me."

"But you said you'd come," she said simply.

In complete faith? Or had this been a test? Pass if he showed, fail if he didn't? Didn't she understand that real life couldn't be set aside so easily? Would she close the café for weeks on end because her mother needed her?

Yeah, he realized. She would.

"I'm here." He couldn't tell her how close a call it had been. Especially not when he felt an overwhelming sense of...rightness. Yeah, that was it.

To hell with real life, he thought violently, even as he knew he didn't mean it. Couldn't afford to mean it.

"Yes." She sighed happily and lifted her face.

Funny thing, given the bruising force of their initial embrace, but this kiss stayed tender. He felt a tearing sense of regret at how close he'd come to disappointing Lucy. He hated the idea that anything he did would hurt her.

Rubbing his cheek on the top of her head, he said hoarsely, "Are you almost done in here?"

"Done?" Lucy pulled back, wild roses blooming in her cheeks, her eyes dazed. She blinked. "Oh. You mean the kitchen. Um… Just give me a minute."

"Can I help?"

She shook her head. "I really was almost done."

He picked up this week's edition of the *Middleton Courier* and sat to read the local gossip while he waited for her, his interest only cursory.

The high school boys' baseball team had failed to make the state playoffs, but the coach was optimistic for next year with so many strong players who had been sophomores and juniors this year. Stephanie Marie English had won a Rotary Club scholarship for a college semester in Rome to study art.

Talk about culture shock for a kid who'd never known anything but Middleton.

A memorial service held for Lucille Burnbaum had been well-attended. The old lady had been ninety-eight, Adrian read, and most recently had been a resident at the Olympic Retirement Home. She left an astonishing number of descendents. He was not at all surprised to see that she'd graduated from Middleton High School back in the thirties.

Did anybody ever *leave* Middleton?

Ignoring the chill he felt, since he hoped like hell Lucy would in fact be willing to leave behind her hometown, Adrian continued to read.

Jeffrey and Ann Peterson welcomed a baby boy, weight six pounds seven ounces. They almost had to be related to Lucy. Good God, how many baby, wedding and Christmas presents did she have to buy?

"I'm ready."

He looked up from the paper, startled at how engrossed he'd become. The kitchen was dark, and she was shrugging on a sweater as she crossed the dining room to him. He studied her as she approached.

Her hair was pulled into a bun, although tiny tendrils straggled after a long day's work. She looked tired, and yet color was still high in her cheeks and her eyes were soft, as though his mere presence made her happy.

His chest hurt again. If this was love, it was damned uncomfortable. Why was he having trouble enjoying the moment, uncomplicated by guilt or a sense of inadequacy or the reminder that he only had until Sunday?

"Good," he said, voice husky.

He followed her home, remembering belatedly that he should have checked in at the B and B. Instead, he took his overnight bag into Lucy's house. He'd claim his room at Samantha's in the morning. If they were really lucky, no one would happen to notice his car parked out front before then.

He gave a grunt of amusement. Yeah, right.

But, hey. Maybe if several relatives chided her about having a man spending the night, it would annoy Lucy enough to give her an added push to make the move to Seattle.

Of course, he had yet to *ask* her if she'd consider moving.

This weekend? Or was it too soon?

Each time he realized what a short time he'd known Lucy, he felt a fresh shock. In his entire adult life, he'd never let anyone be as important to him as she'd become in a matter of weeks.

Inside, she told him somewhat shyly that she needed to take a shower. At her suggestion, he made himself a sandwich and had a glass of milk while he waited. The microwaveable dinner he'd eaten at his desk seemed like a distant memory.

He heard the shower running upstairs, then silence. When she padded barefoot into the kitchen, her face had a rosy hue, her wet hair was loosely braided and she wore a pink chenille robe. The creamy skin and hint of a cleavage revealed at the *V* of the neckline made him wonder if she wore anything beneath the robe. His body immediately tightened.

She smiled at him. "Oh, good. You did find something."

He had to look down at his hand and the remnant of the sandwich to know what she was talking about. "Yeah. Thanks." His gaze swept over her hungrily. "I like you barefoot."

"My toes like it, too." Her eyes were an even deeper blue than usual, suffused with some emotion.

He shoved his plate away and turned the chair, the legs scraping on the floor. "Hey. Come here."

She came to him without hesitation, her cheeks even pinker, but her gaze never leaving his. When she stopped in front of him, he reached up and stroked the smooth, clean line of her throat, continuing down her chest to where the shawl collar crossed. When he untied the robe and slowly parted it, she made no move to resist, only watching his face.

She was naked beneath it, her skin warm and fragrant from the shower, her breasts perfect handfuls, her waist supple and slender, her hips a gentle swell. She quivered with reaction as his hands savored her body.

Adrian had never felt a surge of desire so savage. For a moment he went still, trying to get a grip on himself. "I shouldn't have started this until we'd made it to bed," he said rawly.

"I always did love that scene in *Bull Durham*," she whispered.

He laughed. At least, he thought he did. With one hand he swept the plate and glass from the table, wincing at the sound of glass splintering. Then he lifted her up, the robe open, and sat her butt on the table. One more sight of her body, pale and pretty and sexier than anything he'd ever seen in his life, and he crushed her mouth beneath his.

Her arms clamped around his neck and she kissed him with hunger as ferocious and undeniable.

"You're beautiful," he heard himself say once, in a voice he didn't recognize. The words *I love you* were there, too, but clogged in his throat. He hadn't said them since he was a little boy, and his tongue didn't know how to shape them.

They got his shirt unbuttoned, but not off, his pants open. If he hadn't carried a condom in his wallet, right there, he wouldn't have had the strength of will to go find one. He tried to let her put it on, but thought he'd explode at the tentative touch of her fingers. With a guttural sound he took over, kissing her the whole while, pushing her back down onto the dining-room table. Her legs locked around his waist as he slammed into her in an act so primitive, he'd lost all ability to reason. Sensation rolled atop sensation: creamy skin, gasps, the sharp edge of her teeth, the hot slick glove of her body.

She cried out, spasming, taking him with her. Shockwaves ripped through him, the pleasure so intense he didn't know how he'd live through it and come out unchanged.

He went still as the waves washed out, still holding her with arms that shook. Suddenly unsure his legs would keep holding him, he wrapped her tight and all but fell onto the chair, Lucy straddling him.

They both gasped for breath. Adrian nuzzled his face against the curve where her neck met her shoulder, breathing in her scent. Lavender, maybe; he didn't know. Something flowery but subtle, something Lucy.

"Did you miss me?" she murmured.

His laugh was far more genuine this time, if also as shaken as he felt. "Oh, yeah. You could say that." He kissed the base of her throat, her pulse skittering against his lips. *I love you.* "I don't want to be without you."

"What?" She pulled back to study him with the startled, wary look of a doe surprised around a bend in the trail.

"Do you think—" he cleared his throat "—you could consider moving to Seattle?"

She was silent for a moment, her eyes searching his. "Are you asking me to live with you?" He could hear the constraint in her voice.

"No." He hadn't known what he was going to say

until this moment. "It's probably too soon, but… Ah, I'm asking you to marry me."

"Marry you."

It was killing him that he couldn't tell what she was thinking. "I won't pressure you—"

"Why do you want to marry me?" she asked. "Is it because of…this?" Her glance down encompassed their bodies, half-dressed, flushed with the most intense sex of his life.

"No." He twitched. "Yes, of course, but—" *Say it.* He swallowed, and stepped off into space. "I've never known anyone like you. Anyone with your heart." He laid his fingertips right where it beat, beneath her breast. His voice became scratchy. "I love you."

"Ohhh," she breathed, and suddenly her eyes welled with tears. "I thought— I was afraid—" She pressed her lips together. "I never dreamed—"

"What? Say it."

"That you'd want me forever. I thought this might be…casual for you."

Throat tight, he said, "I'm not a casual man."

"You love me."

"Yeah." He couldn't take his eyes from her face, dominated by those huge blue eyes swelling with tears. "Is there any chance…?"

"Yes!" She laughed even as she cried. "Yes! I think I fell in love with you that first night here, when you looked so stunned."

Grinning foolishly, Adrian devoured the sight of her face. "You'll marry me? You'll at least think about it? I don't want to keep leaving you here. I didn't—" He stopped, stunned by what he'd almost said.

Her head tilted like a curious bird's. "You don't...?"

He tugged her close, so she couldn't see his face. To the top of her head, he finished the sentence. "I didn't like myself without you around." He paused. "I was angry all week."

"Oh, Adrian!" she whispered, wrapping her arms around him and squeezing hard enough to steal the air from his lungs. "I love you. I love you, I love you, I love—"

He surged to his feet and said urgently, "Let's go to bed."

She laughed, even though her cheeks were still wet. "I can walk, you know."

Adrian had the rueful realization that his pants were down around his knees. "I think you'll have to," he admitted, letting her slide down his body to the floor.

She really laughed when she realized what his dilemma was, but he didn't mind. Her laughter never had a bite to it.

"Yeah, yeah," he grumbled in pretend annoyance, and pulled up his pants. The glint of glass caught his eye, and he said, "Ah...I seem to have made a mess."

Tying the belt on her robe, she peered at the dishes and shards of glass scattered on the floor. "I can clean it up in the morning. I don't feel like it right now." She grinned at him. "You can break my glasses anytime you want."

That earned her another kiss, after which she turned out lights as he picked up his overnight bag at the foot of the stairs and went with her to her bedroom.

He detoured to the bathroom to clean up and brush his teeth, returning to her bedroom to find her already in bed, her robe laid over the back of an antique rocking chair.

She smiled at him. "I hope you brought more than one condom."

He lifted a box from his bag. "A man who feels like I do never goes unprepared."

There was that laugh again; no, that giggle, airy and young and heartstoppingly happy.

He had made her happy. Adrian didn't think he'd ever made anyone happy before, outside of triumphs in the courtroom that satisfied his clients.

Somewhere, in the back of his mind, he had the disquieting realization that he didn't want to make Lyle Galbreath happy. The son of a bitch deserved to fry, not to be bailed out to offend again all so that his company could make more money.

That's my job.

He didn't always have to like it.

Maybe tomorrow he'd talk to Lucy. See what she thought. But not now. Now, he was going to make love with her again.

With, he thought, *the woman I'm going to marry.*

He flung his pants over the same chair. Her wide-eyed gaze went to his erection. Then, she lifted the covers to welcome him into her bed.

LUCY AWAKENED in the morning first to the realization that she wasn't alone in bed; her head was pillowed on a warm, solid chest and she seemed to be draped over a man.

Adrian, she thought sleepily, contentedly. She had no immediate inclination to move. From his slow, deep breathing, it was obvious he was still sound asleep. Heaven knows they'd been up a good part of the night.

He loved her. He'd asked her to marry him.

Joy fizzed in her chest, but it wasn't alone. Puzzled, Lucy tried to identify the funny mix of emotions that didn't seem to quite blend.

She was happy. Of course she was. She wished—oh, that she was a little more sure of Adrian, that this wasn't some kind of crazy impulse on his part that had to do with his having found his mother, and him being so certain that no one else in the world would have championed her the way Lucy had. It was as if he'd never met any nice people before. He was so utterly convinced she was special in a way she didn't really think she was. Some people gave their lives to helping the homeless, or children orphaned by AIDS, or…abandoned animals, or any of a thousand important causes. All she'd done was be nice to one gentle, confused, lost woman. It had been practically an *afterthought*. Adrian was bound to realize some day that she was actually pretty average. And then what would happen?

Maybe she was the one who needed to gain confidence, she tried to tell herself. He loved her. Why was she so determined to question his feelings, and so quickly? Because she didn't believe in her good fortune, that someone like him really wanted *her?*

But she didn't think that was it. No matter what Adrian said, she'd never be able to think of herself as beautiful. But he had succeeded in erasing some of her certainty that she was the plain sister. Clearly, *he* didn't see her that way, which pleased her immeasurably.

No, the faintly queasy feeling in her stomach, Lucy realized, had more to do with what all this meant. She'd be selling the café and looking for a job working for someone else, because she couldn't imagine that she could afford or had the resources to start a restaurant in Seattle. And…she'd be moving to Seattle, of course. Adrian had said something about his condo, which meant no garden. Unless they could pick out a house together? A roommate from Lucy's freshman year in college lived in Bellevue, but otherwise she'd be starting all over to create a circle of friends. The idea should be exciting. It *was* exciting! She'd been so sure all her life that she wanted to live somewhere that was more vibrant, more sophisticated. She had been getting awfully set in her ways. What was it she'd thought last week? That she was *contented*. Lucy wasn't sure she liked that word. It sounded middle-aged and stodgy. Wasn't it past time she struck out on a new path, not surrounded by people who'd known her forever? Just think, her family wouldn't be butting in to every decision she made.

Only…what that really meant was that they wouldn't be around at all. They'd keep having the Sunday dinners, but she and Adrian wouldn't make it very often. It was too far to drive more than once a month, tops. And would he want to come at all?

She could still call Sam when she was aggrieved about something, but her sister wouldn't know the people she was talking about. They wouldn't ever have the chance to do a mystery weekend together at the bed-and-breakfast.

Of course, the wedding would be here in Middleton, so she'd be surrounded by family then. And maybe Adrian would take her someplace exotic for a honeymoon. If he could get away from work long enough.

But Lucy felt a peculiar, sinking sensation in her stomach when she imagined herself newly moved into his condominium, and him getting up early and leaving for work. Didn't he say he worked sixty-hour weeks and sometimes more? She would start job hunting, of course, and…she didn't know what else.

Oh, she was being a coward. Imagine, she told herself, him leaving for Seattle without her. Was that any better? Her heart squeezed, and she knew she couldn't bear losing him. This would be an adventure, that's all. She had never planned to stay in Middleton her entire life.

Satisfied, she closed her eyes and snuggled, if such a thing was possible, even closer. She wouldn't wake Adrian up, but she could hardly wait until he did open his eyes. Although she was feeling a little sleepy again.

Lucy was drifting, almost asleep, when the jangle of the telephone ringing made her jerk.

She didn't keep a phone by her bed. Her mother was much too fond of calling before Lucy liked to be up in the morning. She hurriedly slipped out of bed, but saw that Adrian was stirring anyway, blinking and gazing at her with the blank look of someone who hadn't quite placed himself yet.

If it was her mother, she'd kill her. *Especially* if Mom was calling because someone had told her Adrian's car was parked outside her daughter's house all night.

But it wasn't actually that early, Lucy saw, detouring around the broken glass and making it into the kitchen as the answering machine picked up. Lucy hadn't gone to voice mail, because she liked being able to hear who was calling and then decide if she wanted to answer.

"Lucy, this is Dr. Slater. I've already left messages for Adrian on both his cell and home phones. His mother has regained consciousness. I'm hoping you're home and able to make it into the hospital this morning to help orient her. She's pretty confused." He paused. "Give me a call."

Lucy lunged for the phone. "Dr. Slater?"

He'd already hung up.

"Who was that?"

Lucy turned. Adrian was coming down the stairs wearing only jeans. Barefooted and bare-chested, he paused and stretched, his expression one of sleepy-eyed satisfaction.

Still grappling with the news, she said, "That was Dr. Slater. He says…he says your mother has woken up."

Adrian froze a few steps from the bottom. His expression almost broke her heart. For just a moment, he was the little boy who'd come home from the summer in Nova Scotia to find his mommy wasn't there. It was as if he'd heard a sound upstairs, in her bedroom, and hope tore at him even as he knew it probably wasn't her.

He swallowed. "Then I suppose we'd better get dressed and go to the hospital." A muscle in his cheek twitched. "That is…do you have time?"

His courteous question outraged her, but then she recognized it for what it really was: that same little boy bracing himself to do something terribly frightening on his own. Of course he wouldn't plead, but, God, he hoped.

"Don't be silly," she said. "Of course I'm coming. Oh, let's hurry!"

Still looking stunned, Adrian turned and started up the stairs ahead of her.

WHAT IF SHE didn't know him? Never recognized that he was her son, the boy she hadn't seen since she hugged him so fiercely as he was being sent away twenty-three years ago this June?

Adrian moved his shoulders impatiently. She was still his mother. His responsibility. Whether she knew him or not was unlikely to have any impact on the decisions he'd have to make on her behalf. She was mentally ill and unable to adequately care for herself. That was reality. He'd have to find some kind of supervised living situation no matter what.

The wrench in his chest told him he wasn't as dispassionate as he wanted to be. To have found his mother after all these years and then have her fail to remember him… That would hurt.

He could hardly wait to call his grandmother, who was waiting for this moment. She'd taken the news that her long-lost daughter had turned up better than he had feared, saying, "I used to beg God to give me an answer. That was all I asked for. And now I have it."

God, he thought, had chosen to give her more.

Adrian stole a glance at Lucy, who leaned forward as if she could make the car go faster. Thank God for Lucy. No matter what happened, it would be all right with her there. If his mother knew anyone, it would be Lucy.

He took the first spot he saw in the parking lot. Lucy got out as fast as he did, and was ahead of him when they reached the front doors despite his long strides.

"Oh, I can't believe…" she said in a wondering voice, as they went up the elevator.

He laughed in astonishment. "You? You've always believed."

"I think sometimes I pretend."

"You?"

"Well…I am generally optimistic," she admitted. "Half-full."

"Maybe." No one was at the nurses' station, and they were almost to his mother's room. "But you know," Lucy said, "whether you see a glass as half-full or half-empty, the exact same amount of water is in it."

"I'm not so sure." His tone was peculiar even to his own ears. They had turned into the hospital room, and Adrian's stride checked. His heart was drumming.

He heard his own, childish, self-important voice. *When I get home from school today, Mom and me are gonna plant tomatoes. She says she bets mine grow big as this globe!*

How had Mom been both so sad and so optimistic?

Or had she, too, pretended?

Instead of hurrying ahead, Lucy had paused at his side, looking at him in silent inquiry. Seeing his momentary paralysis, she reached over and took his hand, her own so much smaller than his but strong.

He might have hurt her with his desperate grip, but she didn't even wince. For an instant, he squeezed his eyes shut, then gusted out a breath.

"Ready or not," he murmured, and pushed the curtain aside.

CHAPTER THIRTEEN

JUST BEFORE THEY rounded the curtain, Adrian heard Ben Slater talking. "Yes, you're in the hospital. You got hit hard on the head and you've been unconscious."

His tone was infinitely patient, but Adrian guessed he was repeating the information for the umpteenth time.

"My head?" His patient sounded querulous. "Why would they hit my head?"

Adrian's heart lurched. The last time he heard his mother's voice, she'd been waving frantically and calling after the car as it drove away, "Tell *Maman* to let you call me!"

"I will! I will!" he'd yelled back.

Then his father had snapped, "For God's sake, roll up the window."

The curtain swayed as his shoulder brushed it. Adrian came to a stop at the foot of the bed, distantly aware of Dr. Slater, of Lucy still holding tight to his hand, but they were in soft focus at the edges of his vision. What he saw was his mother.

The bed had been cranked up so that she sat nearly upright. She was still too pale, her hair white and unkempt, the IV attached to her hand. But her eyes, the blue only slightly faded from his memory, were open.

With her face now animated, he knew her on a primal level that nearly brought him to his knees.

"Mom," he said hoarsely. *Mommy.*

At the sound of his voice, she turned from the doctor. Her stare was at first uncomprehending, then bewildered; finally he saw alarm then distress that crumpled her face.

"I don't know who you are. Should I?" she appealed to Dr. Slater.

He took her hand and spoke gently. "No. You haven't seen your son in a very long time. He was a little boy the last time you saw him. Now he's all grown up."

"Do I...do I *have* a little boy?" she whispered, studying Adrian furtively.

Disappointment lodged in his throat, making it hard to answer. "Yes. Do you remember? Dad sent me to spend the summer in Nova Scotia with *Maman* and *Grandpère.* You...were gone when I came home. Dad never told me where you went."

"There...there was a little boy." Tears welled in her eyes. "I don't know who he was."

Dr. Slater stepped away, unnoticed. Lucy hung back, letting go of him.

Adrian forced himself to take the last couple of steps, to wrap his hands around the railing. "*I'm* that little boy. Adrian. I grew up."

She searched his face now with a hunger that echoed his own. "You look like someone."

"Dad. Do you remember him? Your husband?"

She shrank back against the pillow, inching away from him. "Am I married? I don't want to be married." Her voice had become more tremulous. "I don't have to be, do I?" she asked the room at large.

Pity gripped him. "No. No, you don't have to be. You haven't been in a very long time. You and Dad got divorced. Do you remember him?" Adrian asked again. "Max Rutledge. He died. I know I look like him."

"You look like someone," she said, in a small frightened voice.

"I wanted to be a ferryboat captain. You took me down almost every day to watch the ferries load and unload. The seagulls would sit on the pilings until the ferry horn sounded, and then they'd screech and soar around it. Sometimes we'd see sea lions. And do you remember the divers? We'd watch their heads bob up."

"It smelled good," she said unexpectedly.

"Yes." Tears burned the back of his eyes, and he, too, could smell the salty, fishy scent of the sound mixed with the exhaust from cars waiting in the ferry line and the aroma of food cooking in the dockside restaurants. For a moment, he wasn't here at all; he was a child again, holding his mother's hand and reveling in the sound of the ferry horn, the sight of water opening between it and the dock, the workers bustling importantly in their bright orange vests as they blocked the wheels of cars and operated the ramp on the dock itself.

Without thought, he held out a hand. His mother slowly, tentatively, lifted her own and laid it in his. It was somehow a shock that his was so large and hers so small instead of the other way around, jarring him from the so-vivid memory. And yet the clasp felt right. They held hands, and they looked at each other, and a knot inside him loosened for the first time in all these years.

"I do remember," she whispered. "That little boy was mine, wasn't he?"

"Yes." He had to clear his throat. "Yes. He was yours."

"But…but who are you then?"

"I'm that little boy, all grown up," he repeated.

Confusion furrowed her brow. "I tried to find him. I know I did."

Choked up, he could only nod.

"I think I tried to go home."

He felt the wetness on his cheeks. "Do you remember your garden? The roses, and the bright blue and purple delphiniums? And your peonies? People would stop their cars to admire the peonies."

"Peonies like manure, you know," she told him. "You have to feed them."

A lump in his throat, he nodded. He did remember. He could almost hear the buzz of honeybees and feel the sun on his face and the carpet of grass he sat on as he watched his mother work in the garden. She often talked, telling him what she was doing and why. He helped her grow seedlings in the small greenhouse attached to the back of the garage. His tomatoes hadn't been quite as big as the globe in his elementary school classroom, but they'd grown fat and red and tasted better than any tomato he'd eaten before or since.

Mom and me grow better tomatoes than anyone, he'd bragged.

"Most plants like to be fed," he said, in a choked voice.

"Do you have peonies in your garden?" she asked.

He used his shirtsleeve to swipe at his cheeks. "I don't have a garden."

Unhappiness deepened every line in her face. "I don't think I do, either. I wish I did."

"Maybe you can again."

Her hand went slack in his. "Who are you?"

He closed his eyes and let her hand go. He was intensely grateful when Dr. Slater stepped forward and said, "You look tired. Perhaps it's time for a nap."

She looked from Adrian to Slater with suspicion and confusion. "Why are you here when I don't know you?"

"I'm the doctor," he said patiently. "You're in the hospital. You hit your head really hard on the pavement."

Lucy came to Adrian's side then. "Elizabeth, I'm so glad to see you awake and talking again. I'm Lucy."

"Of course you're Lucy. Who else would you be?"

Lucy laughed, as naturally as if her sister were teasing her. "Nobody at all. That was a silly thing to say, wasn't it?"

"Yes. I know Lucy," Adrian's mother told the two men.

"Of course you do," Dr. Slater said comfortably.

"Do you have a headache?" Lucy asked.

"I feel…" Her face worked. "I don't know what I feel." She struggled suddenly to sit up straighter and grabbed for the bars. "My cart! Where's my cart? Did somebody take my things?"

"No. No, all your things are at my house. Do you remember crossing the highway to go to Safeway? You were hit by a car. I took everything home to be sure it stayed safe while you got better here in the hospital."

It went on that way: comprehension, bewilderment, all answered by Lucy's steady warmth and reassurance. Adrian backed away from the bed, drained, stunned by how much he felt for this frightened, prematurely aged woman who could summon only fleeting memories of him, her son.

Lucy sent him away to get breakfast. He went back

to her place, showered and packed his overnight bag again. About to close her front door behind him, he turned around and went back to the bedroom where she stored his mother's paltry belongings. He picked through, taking a few things he thought might mean something to her.

Ten minutes later, he checked in at the bed-and-breakfast.

As he was signing the book, Samantha watched him with a frown puckering her forehead. The expression was startlingly like Lucy's when she was perturbed.

"Are you all right?"

All right? Adrian didn't know. The ground beneath his feet had shifted.

"My mother regained consciousness. Lucy's at the hospital. I'm going back as soon as I—" For a moment he couldn't remember what he was supposed to be doing. "I don't suppose you're still serving breakfast."

"Not officially, but I'll put something together for you," she said immediately. "Why don't you drop your bag off upstairs and then come to the dining room?"

Samantha's "something" turned out to be scrambled eggs, thick slabs of whole wheat toast smothered in homemade blackberry jam and pastries that melted in his mouth. Adrian ate as if he were starving, which seemed to please her.

He went back to the hospital to release Lucy, who murmured, "Ssh, she's napping." One of the gift-shop volunteers had offered her a ride home, she said. "So you can stay." She kissed him on the cheek, then added, "I'll try to pop in midafternoon, between the lunch and dinner crowds," before she departed. She didn't question the small carton he carried.

His mother's sleep was more peaceful than the coma had been, although the similarity was great enough that Adrian couldn't seem to tear his eyes from her. Sitting there at the bedside, he couldn't help wondering whether people ever slipped back into comas. What if she never opened her eyes again?

An hour passed. Two. Where the hell was Slater? Adrian wondered angrily.

Having breakfast. Or lunch, as late as it was. Shaving.

Adrian rubbed a hand over his own stubble. Should have done that himself. He didn't want to scare her.

A nurse came in several times, checking monitors. He was touched when she brought him coffee from the cafeteria.

He was taking a swallow of it when he realized his mother's eyes were open. She stayed very still and stared at him with all the alarm of a wild creature cornered.

"You're awake," he said, careful to speak quietly. "You're in the hospital. Do you remember getting hit by the car?"

"I don't want to be in the hospital! I don't like hospitals!" She sat up and grabbed for the bed rail, her gown slipping to bare a protuberant collarbone. "Let me out!"

He hit the Call button, and with the nurse's help calmed his mother.

He had to explain all over again who he was.

"I did have a little boy," she said again, eyeing him with deep suspicion.

"I brought pictures." He opened the carton he'd set

at his feet, hoping this was the right thing to do. He regretted having left her driver's license and that long-ago Mother's Day card at his condo in Seattle. But he handed her a school photo of him that she'd kept all these years and watched her stare down at it.

After a moment she lifted her gaze from the picture, examined his face minutely, then returned to the photograph.

"Yes, that's really me," Adrian said.

She looked at the other pictures, including the one of herself as a girl. That one she stared at the longest.

Adrian talked, telling her about her parents and the home in Nova Scotia where she'd grown up.

"I can't remember how to get there," she said sadly.

He had to swallow several times before he could speak. "I know."

After a minute he lifted the conch shell from the box and saw her smile. He set it on the bed beside her.

"I always wanted one of those," she confided. "I tried to bring one home once, from Hawaii. But *he* wouldn't let me. He said it was too big." Her eyes clouded with the memories. "I found that one at a garage sale. Imagine! They were selling it for two dollars."

"You were lucky."

"Lucky?" She nodded, stroking the satiny interior. "Sometimes I am, you know."

His heart was damn near breaking. "You were lucky to meet Lucy." Or was he the lucky one, because she'd brought Lucy into *his* life?

"Do you know Lucy?" His mother gazed at him in surprise. "She has me to lunch often. We're good friends."

"I know you are." He smiled at her. "Lucy said she'd

be by for a visit this afternoon, between her lunch and dinner crowd."

Her face brightened. "Have you eaten her soup? It's very good."

Adrian agreed that he had. He got her talking about meals she'd eaten at the café, and told her he'd met Father Joseph. His mother confided that she didn't really like to listen to sermons, but she did enjoy the children. "And they need me," she told him with simple satisfaction. Her forehead creased. "This isn't Sunday, is it? Because they count on me."

"No, it's Saturday. And they know you won't be there tomorrow, since you're in the hospital. Some of the other mothers are filling in."

"Oh."

Back and forth. One minute she remembered, the next she was confused. Adrian was handicapped by not knowing what she'd been like before the accident. She hadn't remembered her past, or had professed not to. So, okay; that part might *be* normal for her. But he guessed the present had been in clearer focus for her, or she wouldn't have remembered the classified ads for garage sales and which started on Friday and which on Saturday, that *this* day was Sunday and she needed to be at the church, and so on.

Slater did show up and examined her, then talked to Adrian privately in the hall.

"Her mental acuity is actually quite remarkable considering." He shook his head in apparent admiration, his cherubic face glowing with delight.

"She's still pretty confused."

"Wouldn't you be?" the doctor said simply. "And

yes, I feel confident she'll be back to herself in no time, champing at the bit to be out of the hospital."

Remembering her panic, Adrian said, "She doesn't like hospitals."

"If your father did commit her…"

God, yes. This bed, with the railings that looked like bars, might feel like prison to her. "Lucy says that most of the time she refused the offer of places to stay."

"Because she didn't like being obligated?" Slater rocked on his heels, thinking. "Or because she feels trapped if she's indoors for any length of time?"

Adrian shook his head, mute. His own mother, and he knew next to nothing about what was going on in her head.

"Perhaps this is a good time to evaluate her mental-health issues," the doctor suggested. "She might make further improvement on an appropriate drug regimen."

Adrian nodded numbly. "Yes, in a few days."

Slater clapped him on the back. "Give her time before you make any decisions."

Watching him stride down the hall, Adrian thought bleakly, *What choice do I have?* She obviously couldn't take care of herself.

Lucy came again and went, as did Father Joseph, whom she'd called with the news. Adrian used his visit to have a hurried dinner in the cafeteria before return-ing to his mother's bedside. The nurse greeted him with relief.

"She's agitated when you're gone."

"I keep having to explain again who I am."

She gave him a gentle smile he would once have interpreted as pitying. "But I think maybe, deep inside, she *knows*."

Lucy came for him after she closed the café. By then his mother was sleeping. He stood wearily, and they both looked down at her.

Lucy's hand crept into his. "Today felt like a miracle," she said softly.

Did it? He moved his shoulders to ease knotted muscles. Maybe. His mother *had* remembered him, if only through the haze of a great distance.

He couldn't claim his memories of her were much sharper. Bits and pieces kept coming to him, but he'd been dismayed to realize how much he had shut out, either to please his father or in self-defense. Most recalled memories were good, but today, as he had patiently explained yet again who he was, he'd suddenly remembered walking in the door from school one day, just like any other day until then, to have her start violently at the sight of him and stare at him with wild eyes. She'd cried, "Go away! I won't listen to you! You're not there. You're not! You're not!"

"Mommy?" he had whispered in fright. "It's me. Adrian. Who are you talking to?"

"Nobody! I won't listen!" Clapping her hands over her ears, she had whirled and run from the kitchen, shutting herself in her bedroom. He had gazed longingly at the phone, wanting to call his father and say, "There's something wrong with Mom." But he hadn't, because...

He didn't know why, just that his *job* was to shield his mom from everyone. Even Dad.

Especially Dad, Adrian thought now, in the hospital. He wondered whether she'd been on medication in those days. Whether she'd resisted taking it. Whether his father had been scared for him, coming home after school to her. In his own way, had he thought he was doing the right thing?

Maybe, Adrian thought again. If only his father had talked to him, if not then, later.

"You'll follow me home?" Lucy asked, her hand still in his as they rode the elevator down.

He studied her face. In the harsh white hospital lighting, she looked like she had bruises beneath her eyes. Freckles stood out in heightened relief. Neither of them had slept much last night, and the phone call from Slater had come early this morning.

"You look exhausted."

"I am tired, but—"

"I checked in to the B and B," he reminded her. "My stuff's there. Samantha will expect me."

She frowned at him. "Why did you do that?"

"Because I was trying to protect you from gossip. I'd made the reservations last week, you know."

"I don't care what my family thinks."

They'd reached her car and stopped. Running his hands up and down her arms, which were bare despite the cool night air, Adrian said roughly, "Are you sure?"

"Of course I'm sure," she snapped, just vehemently enough he didn't believe her.

"We're both tired," he said. "Why don't you come to Sam's for breakfast in the morning?"

After a moment she dipped her head, her expression still sulky. "Oh, fine."

He kissed her, feeling extraordinary tenderness. It heartened him that she was prepared to defy her family for him, although he was discovering that he didn't like the idea of their disapproval. He didn't want her to lose more than she had to, only because she'd made the decision to love him.

He drove behind her—stupid as it was, considering she'd been getting herself home without his protection for years—then pulled to the curb until he saw her unlock her front door, give a wave and disappear inside. He looped back to her sister's, where it appeared everyone had gone to bed. A note taped to the stair newel told him about the snack he could help himself to in the kitchen if he was hungry.

A tired grin pulled at his mouth as he turned that way instead of starting up the stairs. The Peterson sisters did like to feed people.

THANK GOODNESS the café was closed the next two days. Lucy spent most of them at the hospital with Adrian.

She liked that he'd brought the conch shell to his mother. It was something she'd loved, and was better than flowers, although he did bring those, too. Sunday he called a florist in Port Angeles and had a huge bouquet of peonies delivered. The hat lady cried. When she grabbed her son's hands and pulled him close until his forehead rested against hers, Lucy eased out of the room. She waited for several minutes then wiped tears from her eyes before she went back in.

He did come home with her Sunday and Monday nights both, but wouldn't stay to sleep.

"Sam won't know," she protested one night.

"Yes, she will. She leaves me a snack every night."

"Maybe you weren't hungry. Maybe you got up and left early."

He laughed. "Who'd turn down anything either of

you have cooked? And there's no way I'd get up earlier than she does. I swear she's already in the kitchen baking by six."

Lucy made a face. "She always liked mornings."

"But you don't?"

They hadn't actually had a chance to find out things like that about each other, she realized. She didn't know if he was usually grumpy in the morning, or unbearably cheerful, whether he normally needed six hours of sleep a night or nine.

"My alarm never woke me. When I was in high school, Mom always had to yell until she got mad to make sure I was up." She grinned at him. "You notice I don't make breakfast at the café."

That was one of the nice things about those couple of days. His mom tired easily, then the two of them could talk, sometimes quietly at her bedside, sometimes in the cafeteria.

Monday morning Lucy overheard part of a terse phone call he made. He sounded unhappy, and she was a little chilled by his remote expression when he turned and saw her.

"Work?" she asked.

He gave a short nod. "This is not a good time for me to go missing in action."

"Is there ever a good time?"

Adrian grimaced. "No."

Then he changed the subject, and she didn't try to pursue the question of when he would have to go back to Seattle.

The hat lady was better each day, more herself. Of course she was weak from being in bed so long. First she made it shakily to the bathroom; by Monday evening, she was able to walk slowly up and down the hall. She was eating, and even reading after the librarian visited and left her a couple of books.

Lucy could tell Adrian was frustrated that she was remembering her life in Middleton but not much about before. He wanted to know where she'd been in the intervening years. He wanted her to remember *him* better than she did.

Tuesday morning he came to Lucy's house for breakfast, then they drove separately to the hospital. When they walked into his mother's room and he said, "Hi, Mom," she gave him a surprised glance.

In an upper-crust British accent, she asked, "Who are you?"

He swore under his breath. "I'm your son, Adrian. Don't you remember? Last night you told me what my first word was—"

"Yes, I answered you last night. No, this morning, sir, I say."

He stared at her, baffled. "What in the hell?"

Lucy squeezed his forearm and murmured in his ear, "I think she's Elizabeth Barrett Browning again. The poet?" she said, when he stared uncomprehendingly at her.

"My God. She's crazy."

"Don't say that in front of her." Lucy turned and marched out of the room, aware when he followed. She swung to face him. "I told you what she's like."

"Damn it, even though she's been confused, she's been herself," he all but yelled at her. "Why this? Why now?"

"Because she's getting better."

He shook his head and kept shaking it. "This is *better?*"

"It's who she's been for a long time," Lucy tried to explain.

Intense frustration on his face, he said, "I don't have time for this. I've got to get back to Seattle today."

"Back to Seattle?" Lucy echoed. "You didn't say—"

His expression changed. "I got another call on the way over here. I don't have any choice. I'll try to make it back Friday."

"But…what if she's ready to be discharged before then?"

He gave a short, harsh laugh. "You're kidding, right? I've talked to Slater. I've told him I'll be making arrangements for her."

It was the way he said *arrangements,* so chilly, so… final.

Something heavy settled in Lucy's chest. She felt stupid. She'd built some kind of castle in the air where he was concerned. He'd never been the man she thought he was; he couldn't be if he could stick to a decision he'd made back at the beginning before he'd known his mother at all.

Before he'd known Middleton, and Lucy.

CHAPTER FOURTEEN

SHE'D BEEN AWARE from the beginning that Adrian had some kind of nursing home in mind. Of course if his mother hadn't come out of the coma she'd have had to be cared for. Why, Lucy asked herself, hadn't she realized he was going ahead with his plan even as the hat lady recovered?

Still standing there in the hospital corridor, she said, "You're not going to let her stay in Middleton?"

"Living on the street?" He looked at her as if *she* were crazy.

"She did okay," Lucy mumbled. Maybe it wasn't the best solution, she could see why he balked, but she hated the other possibilities, too.

"She won't have you anymore," he said, in the tone of an adult pointing out the obvious to a child. "Wouldn't you rather she was in Seattle where you can see her?"

The pain in her chest was so great, she could hardly breathe. This man staring at her with such impatience seemed like a stranger. Could she really leave Middleton and everyone else in the world she loved to share her life with him? The fact that he hadn't given any thought at all to what would make his mother happiest bothered her terribly.

Would he make decisions like that for her, too? Lucy wondered. Yes, he was taking responsibility. Yes, he was doing what he considered right. All without the slightest hint of compassion or understanding. Was he more like his father than he would admit to being?

"Why are you looking at me like that?" His attention was torn away when the cell phone she hadn't even realized he was carrying rang, and he flipped it open to read the caller's number. Snapping it shut, he said, "I've really got to go. We can talk about this later." He nodded toward the elevator. "Walk me down?"

"You aren't going to say goodbye?"

His jaw flexed. "Miss Browning doesn't even know who I am. She isn't going to miss me."

Lucy lifted her chin. "No, I think I'll stay here with her."

That frustration flashed across his face again. "Think about it. You'll see that I'm right." When she didn't respond, he added a clipped, "I'll call."

Lucy took a step toward the room so that he didn't try to kiss her. Right this moment, she couldn't bear to have him touch her. "Drive carefully."

"I know this isn't ideal…." He frowned, looking like the man she'd first met when she tracked him down in Seattle: impatient, emotionally distant, prepared to dismiss her.

I didn't like myself without you around. He'd paused, then added with seeming reluctance, *I was angry all week.*

Maybe, she thought in a kind of horror, *that's who he really is.*

He said something else; probably repeated, "I'll call."

She stood there and watched him walk away, very likely already putting her and his mother out of his mind.

No, that wasn't fair. He'd said, "I love you."

Tears burning in her eyes, Lucy whispered, "What if I *don't* see that you're right?"

FOR ONCE, HER MOTHER had knocked. When Lucy answered the door, Helen said rather tentatively, "May I come in?"

"You don't have to ask." She tried very hard to wipe all signs of unhappiness from her face. It was bad enough that her mother would ask about the dark smudges under her eyes. She'd hardly slept at all last night.

"I'm not the one who usually barges in." Her mom followed her in and they headed toward the kitchen. They always talked in the kitchen; that's where Martin women felt the most comfortable. "That's your aunt Marian."

"*And* Aunt Lynn. *And* Aunt…"

Laughing, her mother said, "Okay, okay! We don't stand on ceremony in this family."

"Tea?"

"Please." She pulled out a kitchen chair and sat.

Lucy couldn't help remembering what she and Adrian had done on that very table. Biting her lip, she turned her back as she ran hot water into the teakettle. Some things, parents didn't need to know.

"So what's up?" she asked casually, once she'd set mugs out on the counter.

"I think that's my question." Her mother's gaze took in the exhaustion on her face, and more. "I've been worried about you."

Adrian had left only yesterday. How could her mother know to worry?

"Why?" Lucy asked.

"You haven't talked to me at all lately. Even your father guessed you'd fallen for Adrian. The fact that you haven't said anything has made me wonder—"

"Wonder?" she echoed, faintly.

Her mother's voice was gentle. "Oh, whether he reciprocates your feelings. Or whether you're afraid he doesn't."

Just like that, tears were rolling down her cheeks. With shaking hands, she swiped at them. "Oh, Mom!"

Her mother was out of the chair in an instant and had her arms around Lucy, holding her as she cried. "Oh, sweetie," she murmured. "Oh, sweetie, I'm so sorry."

Lucy sobbed until the teakettle whistled, then went to the bathroom to wash her face and compose herself while her mother poured the tea. She'd already carried the mugs to the table and was waiting when Lucy returned.

"How can he be such an idiot?" Helen said furiously, the minute Lucy had sat down. "Not to love you the way you deserve."

"Mom, that isn't it." So quickly, tears threatened again. By sheer force of will, she managed to hold them back. Or perhaps she'd run out of tears. "He says he loves me." She hesitated. "He asked me to marry him, Mom."

Her mother gaped at her. "And you didn't tell me?"

"Everything happened so fast. It was the next morning that his mom came out of her coma and—"

Helen's eyes narrowed. "And you weren't sure you were going to say yes."

"I did say yes." And oh, it hurt to remember her joy. Taking a deep breath, she told her mother everything:

her hopes, her doubts, her fears. "Am I crazy?" she begged at the end.

Her mother's expression was sorrowful. "Are you sure he isn't right about the hat lady? I mean, look what happened to her."

Lucy bristled. "Anybody could have been hit crossing the highway."

"Yes, of course. But you can't tell me you weren't already worried about her. I was shocked to hear that she's only in her fifties. Her diet is terrible, most nights she has no shelter. You've done your best for her, but—"

Her throat closed. "Was it good enough? Is that what you're asking?"

"I'm not suggesting you could or should have done more. Lucy, what you did for her was extraordinary. I'm simply asking if she might not be better off where she's taken care of."

"Can you imagine her in a room in a nursing home? Maybe sharing with someone else. Able to go out only under supervision." Her voice shook. "Those places lock their doors, Mom."

Her mother was silent for a moment, her eyes troubled. "No," she said at last. "No, I can't. She's a little bit like a wild creature. But, unlike you, I can see why Adrian might believe he's doing the right thing."

Lucy slumped. "I can, too. It isn't really his decision that bothers me. It's the way he came to it. He didn't even talk to me, Mom. He'd made up his mind before he got here that first night, and he never even considered changing it. She'd made herself a life here, one she chose. Surely there was a way to compromise."

Her mother held up her hand. "Don't get mad at me.

I agree. And I can see why you can't marry a man who won't talk over big decisions with you, and actually *listen* to you."

"Oh, Mom." With no warning, the tears spilled over this time. "I wish I didn't love him!"

Her mother scooted her chair around to Lucy's side of the table so she could once again hold her. "I know," her mother murmured. "I know."

ADRIAN DID CALL that week, although once again he sounded harried and...different. He wasn't her Adrian, he was the impatient, guarded man Lucy had met that first day, when she walked into his office. The one who'd wanted to believe she was lying to him, for reasons she couldn't imagine.

What must it be like, to always assume the worst about people?

She'd have sworn she had discovered who he really was beneath that hard veneer, but now she wondered. He'd been only ten years old when his mother disappeared from his life. A little boy. He'd had over twenty years to be influenced by his father, to take on the habits and mind set that made him who he was. Probably she'd been naive, even foolish, to believe he could somehow shed those aspects of himself, as if he were wriggling out of his skin and leaving it behind, just because he'd recovered childhood memories, found his mother.

Found me.

He did say, the first time he called, "I know you're upset with me, but you have to look at reality, Lucy."

"We had a real life before you came to Middleton."

She tried so hard to sound as calm as he did, but her voice defied her by trembling. "It wasn't so bad."

He was silent for so long, she almost cracked and started babbling, conceding him anything he wanted.

But at last he said, "I'm getting the feeling you wish you'd never come looking for me."

She squeezed her eyes shut, willing herself not to cry. "I didn't say that. I wouldn't. She needs you, and you need her."

"What about you?" he asked softly. "What do you need?"

"For you to talk to me," she whispered, remembering everything she and her mother had said. "To really talk to me."

"What do you think I'm doing now?" he snapped. He sounded ragged, even angry. He muttered something she took as an expletive. "I want to see you, but I can't get away until the weekend. Can we put this on hold until then?"

Did that mean his decision wasn't final? Hope, fragile but still alive, stirred in her. That he might actually listen this time?

"Yes. Okay," she said. "I'm here."

At last, Adrian's voice softened. "I wish I was there with you. Or you were here with me."

Would she have wanted to be there in Seattle with him? Probably home alone in his condo, which she pictured as ultramodern, with chrome and neutral colors and none of the messiness her idea of real life produced. If she were there, they'd still be talking on the phone, because he'd be in his office.

But she knew suddenly she didn't care.

Yes, she had made discoveries of her own these past weeks. Perhaps, in showing Middleton to Adrian, she'd seen it anew herself. However it had happened, she knew now that she loved her hometown. She loved living here, knowing her customers, knowing her neighbors, feeling her family's love and support behind her. If she could, she'd travel—she did want to see more of the world. But she wanted to be able to come home again. Starting all over in a new place wasn't the adventure she'd yearned for. Loving someone, trusting him, taking the risk of giving so much of herself to him, *that* was the real adventure.

And for that, she'd leave Middleton in a heartbeat. If Adrian really was the man she'd fallen in love with, she couldn't imagine wanting to be anywhere he wasn't. She was good at making friends. She could build a satisfying career, pursue hobbies, perhaps talk him into buying a house where she could garden. And he would come home to her every night, however tired, however frustrated by his day. They'd talk, they'd make love, they'd start a family of their own.

Her choice would be him, with no hesitation. If he was the man she wanted so desperately to believe he was.

"I wish that, too," she admitted.

His voice lowered to a rumble. "I'll see you this weekend. I promise. If things work out the way I think they will…" He paused, and she heard a woman's voice in the background. Carol, no doubt.

Carol, who was the one who'd been looking for the assisted-living home for his mother. Carol, who didn't even know the hat lady.

He came back on. "I've got to go. I'll see you this weekend. Friday, if I can get away, otherwise Saturday."

"Yes. Okay."

He didn't say "I love you." Lucy supposed he didn't want to, with Carol standing there.

But, setting down the phone, she found the absence of the words bothered her. It seemed symbolic. The arrogant, hard Adrian Rutledge, attorney-at-law, wouldn't let anybody see him being soft.

Still, he *had* implied that they still had time to talk, that there might be room for negotiation. So she would let herself feel hopeful. Because he did love her. She believed that much.

"YOU'RE TAKING HER, just like that?"

Lucy didn't even know why she was in shock. Yes, she did—she'd foolishly imagined that he was promising her something that apparently had never crossed his mind.

When he said, "Can we put this on hold?" he hadn't meant that there was still time to talk about his mom's future. He'd probably thought he could pacify her in person. Or else he hadn't understood that his decision wasn't just about how happy or unhappy the hat lady would be, but was also about him.

This scene had begun playing out last week, and all it was doing now was concluding. She was the idiot, thinking that, because his voice had softened, she'd gotten through to him. Apparently she'd been an idiot all along, believing that once he knew his mother he'd slow down and think about what would give her the best quality of life.

Instead, he scowled at her. "What do you mean, *just like that?* I let you know last night that I was coming."

Yes, he had. She'd found a message on her phone at

home when she got in at nearly midnight after closing the restaurant.

I got lucky and found an opening for Mom at a great place. I've already called Slater. I'll be over in the morning to get her. Meet me at the hospital? Say, eleven?

Too late to call him back, or so she told herself. He couldn't mean it. Or…was there any chance he'd gotten his mom a bed at the nursing home here in Middleton as a temporary measure, and that he wanted to surprise her?

Dumb, dumb, dumb, she told herself now.

"She's going to be so scared."

"More scared than she was living on the street?" He snorted, as if she were being ridiculous. After a pause, he conceded, "It'll be an adjustment."

Her face felt stiff; her voice came out wooden. "Why didn't you just have her transported in an ambulance? Or a helicopter? And saved yourself the trip?"

He moved his shoulders. "I, uh, liked the idea of us riding the ferry together. I thought…she might be excited."

For a moment her heart quivered. The man she'd fallen in love with was still in there. But then she imagined the hat lady in a room at an assisted-living facility where the doors were undoubtedly locked. She would have no freedom at all.

"The place has a garden." Adrian sounded tentative. "Her room looks out on some roses."

Lucy swallowed a lump in her throat. "Can she go out? Maybe take walks?"

She saw the answer on his face. Sucking in a breath, she told him, "I said goodbye to your mom already. I just waited to—"

"Tell me what you thought?"

She gave a twisted smile. "Something like that."

He reached a hand out to her, his voice gruff, urgent. "Lucy... I know I said we'd talk, but I can't get back until next weekend. Friday night—"

She backed away, not meeting his eyes. "Don't bother."

He flinched. "So in the end this is about my mother."

"No." Lucy shook her head and took one last, agonizing look at his lean face and the turmoil in his eyes. In a choked voice, she said, "It's about you." Then she turned and fled.

Through the haze of tears, she had no idea whether people were staring as she hurried out of the elevator and crossed the lobby then the parking lot. She knew only that Adrian didn't follow.

ALL ABOUT HIM? Adrian thought incredulously. Who was she kidding?

His fingers flexed on the steering wheel as he followed the line of weekend traffic. In the end, it was really all about her. Or maybe it was about his mother. Was Lucy making the point that, while he might be Elizabeth Rutledge's son, she still knew her best?

Feeling sick, he thought, *It's true.* But what in hell did she think he should do? Walk Mom to the hospital door and wave cheerily as she pushed her shopping cart toward the highway then God knows where? She was fifty-six years old. She had multiple personalities. Letting her continue to live on the street wasn't an option.

"I don't know this place." Beside him, Elizabeth's voice quavered. She gripped the armrest so hard, her knuckles shone white. "Where are we going?"

They hadn't even reached the Hood Canal Bridge, and he'd already repeated himself twenty or so times. But he smiled reassuringly anyway and said, "Remember? We're going to ride on the ferry."

"And then you're taking me home. Right?"

"Don't you *want* to ride on the ferry? Remember when we used to do that? We'd walk on, and go outside so the wind blew on our faces. Well, this time we're driving the car on."

She stiffened. "That doesn't look like a ferry."

The highway emerged from a long curve to reveal the bridge ahead, the broad canal sparkling beneath.

He explained that they still had an hour's drive.

"When will we be home?"

What, in her mind, was home? Adrian wondered. The hospital? One of her hideouts? The church? Middleton in general?

"Remember, I talked to you about the new place you'll be living."

"I don't want a new place." She was definite about that. "I don't think I want to ride on the ferry, not if you won't take me home."

"Remember the accident? You still need extra care. You're not very strong yet, Mom."

"Father Joseph always lets me stay in my room at the church. I can do that. Or Lucy. Lucy would let me stay."

Goddamn it. She probably would. But Adrian couldn't foist his problems on Lucy. Not now, when it was clear she didn't love him. Not really, not the way he'd believed when he had been riding on a powerful wave of hope.

And it wasn't as if she'd ever offered, he realized, his

thoughts crystalline and sharp-edged. The anger he clung to was keeping the agony at bay, but it was there, barely hiding around the corner. He focused on the anger, shutting out the grief. Until he got his mother settled, he couldn't afford to break down.

Yeah, Lucy wanted him to find a solution, but she'd never suggested an alternative. Apparently he was supposed to have figured out a perfect answer—which, of course, she already knew, but hadn't shared with him. Maybe it had been a test, one he'd failed. Well, to hell with her, he thought, teeth clenched, and knew he didn't mean it.

"I don't know where we are," his mother repeated. Her frightened gaze swung from the landscape to him. "I want to go back now!"

Gripping the steering wheel so hard he swore the plastic groaned, Adrian explained again. And again. And again.

CHAPTER FIFTEEN

STILL CLENCHING the steering wheel, Adrian tried to count his blessings. At least his mother was herself today, not Queen Elizabeth or the poet. She was definitely in the here and now. Adrian tried to be glad.

Lucy had packed his mother's pitiful store of belongings into a couple of suitcases, which he suspected she'd bought for the occasion. His mother had already been dressed when he arrived at the hospital, wearing a pretty flowered dress with a wide belt, comfortable shoes and a hat, one of those small oval ones that perched rakishly atop her head, edged by net that dipped over her forehead. It made him think of Audrey Hepburn.

He grimaced. No, if she glanced in a mirror she'd see Elizabeth Taylor, he supposed.

With only another dozen repetitions of the same conversation, they made it to Poulsbo, then onto Bainbridge Island, and finally to the ferry landing. She fell silent briefly when they drove on, the ramp rattling beneath the tires, and the ferry workers directed him to park on one side. Adrian set the brake and turned off the engine, then closed his eyes briefly. His neck and shoulders were so tight, he wasn't sure he could unbend enough to unlatch the door or get out.

After a minute, he said, "Shall we go up? I always liked watching the ferry pull away from the dock."

"We won't get off, will we? We'll ride it over and back, the way we always did. That might be fun."

He unfastened her seat belt and his own, and got out of the car. Panic was building in his chest. What happened when they got to the other side? Would she fight him? How the hell could he leave her at the assisted-living place if she was terrified or crying?

He heard Lucy's voice in his head. *Did you ask* her *what she wants?*

He didn't have to. He knew. She wanted to return to her familiar small-town streets, her familiar routine. Garage sales on Friday and Saturday mornings, the church day care on Sundays, the library, the hair salon, Safeway and the Pancake Haus and Lucy's café.

Grimy, pushing her stolen shopping cart, inviting pity and charity.

Adrian held open the heavy door for his mother. She climbed the steps slowly, holding up everyone else. Once on the passenger deck, she had to sit immediately, looking pale and alarmingly fragile.

Would she be happier at the Middleton assisted-living facility, even if she'd be confined there, too, and he couldn't see her very often?

But Lucy would be there. Not with him in Seattle the way he'd dreamed. Believed she would be.

He realized, as his mother shakily rose and leaned on his arm so they could proceed slowly toward the back of the ferry and the outdoor deck that looked down on the still loading cars and the dock, that he was as bewildered as she was.

He'd caught one of the first ferries that morning, eager to arrive. Of course he'd only see Lucy briefly, but he could kiss her, talk to her, make plans. He'd go back next weekend.

But the minute he saw her, he knew something was wrong. She'd looked at him as if he were a stranger. When he tried to remember all the things she'd said, they blurred.

He did remember one accusation. "I thought you were getting to know *her*. But you never saw her as a person, did you? Only as she related to you."

His mother wrapped her hands around the railing and leaned against it, her head lifted for a minute, her eyes closed, as a breeze toyed with her white curls. She breathed in as though the salty air tasted like fine wine. For that brief instant, apparently oblivious to the chattering family who had joined them out here, she looked at peace.

She had always been fragile. As long as Adrian could remember, he had wanted to shield her from the world. Was that so bad?

"That summer I went to visit *Maman* and *Grandpère* in Nova Scotia, where did you go?" he asked.

Her eyes opened and she turned her head. After a minute, she said in a voice so soft he had to bend closer to hear, "It was a hospital. I think. He said I'd get better."

"Did you?"

"They made me feel so cloudy." Her eyes pleaded with him for understanding. "I wasn't *me*. I don't know who I was. I don't like hospitals."

"Where did you go after you left the hospital?"

Her forehead crinkled in puzzlement. "I tried to go home, but I couldn't find it."

"Home to me in Edmonds, or to your parents?"

The ferry horn sounded, making them both jump. The gulls cried and swooped overhead the way he remembered from when he was a boy. She looked away, watching the water churn between them and the dock. "I don't know. There was someplace I thought I should go. But I couldn't."

He felt sick, imagining her homeless, frightened, unable to remember even how to call her own mother.

"I missed you," he said quietly, past the lump in his throat.

"I thought you were still a little boy. I'm not sure how you can be my Adrian."

"I am." He smiled at her, although the effort hurt. "I still love to ride the ferry."

"I think I have to sit down," she said. "If you don't mind."

"Of course I don't."

He found them a seat inside by the window, and watched her gaze hungrily out at the sailboats chasing each other, the barge moving slowly to the south, the water a bright blue with the sun almost directly overhead.

He could take her on outings. To restaurants and parks and to the beach. When she was stronger, they could fly to Nova Scotia. He wondered if she might even want to stay there, at least for now. Except *Maman* was a very old woman now, not able to care for her.

But the people in Middleton had. He thought they might be happy to continue to do so, except for the grumpy few who had always disdained her, their one-and-only homeless person.

She wouldn't have to be homeless. He could cer-

tainly afford to rent her a room, or even buy her a house
if she wanted one.

Yes, but could she be trusted to live alone? What if
she left a burner or curling iron or God knew what on,
or a faucet running? What if she locked herself out on
a cold night, or forgot where she lived, or…?

As if Lucy were sitting there beside him, he heard her
say, "She's not senile, you know. Do you think that
parents would trust her with their children if she were?
Or that she could enjoy reading the way she does, and
discussing the themes? That she could keep appointments? She's remarkably well-organized, actually. And
she has such a good memory for the names of authors
whose books she's loved, and perennials and old roses,
and historical figures."

Had she said that, when she was trying to persuade
him to make a different plan? Adrian wasn't sure.

Suddenly he felt sick. Had he made the right decision? Had it ever been the right one for his mother?

He felt a yawning emptiness inside and identified it.
He didn't want to lose her again, and he thought he would
if he gave her back to Middleton. But the truth was, she
wasn't the mom he remembered anyway. Oh, she was still
that, in flickers of memory, but those were overlaid by the
life she'd chosen since. One that hadn't been so bad.

Would Lucy have him back if he took his mom home
to Middleton? The tearing pain in his gut told him no.
It was too late. He'd done something wrong. Or maybe
it was just who he was. Nobody since his mother had
ever loved him. Why had he believed Lucy could?

But maybe, just maybe, he could make things right
for the hat lady.

It seemed symbolic that they were seated to be looking back rather than forward, at the approaching cityscape. Turning his face away from the window, telling himself his eyes burned from the bright reflection of the sun on the water and not from emotion, Adrian thought, *I want to go back, too. I want to be part of a family, part of a town.*

He had responsibilities. Clients.

Did he give a damn about a one of them?

I can't move to Middleton if Lucy doesn't want me.

No, but he could change his life. He could accept the lessons she and his mother had taught.

And…it wouldn't hurt to explore possibilities, would it? In case he hadn't been wrong about Lucy?

Still hurting but also feeling a fragile renewal of the precious hope Lucy had given him, he said, "Mom, I'm sorry I dragged you on this trip."

She smiled sunnily at him. "I'm fine, Adrian. You were right. This *was* fun. Although I am looking forward to going home."

He smiled at her wryly. "I know."

Crazy or not, his mother was on to something. Middleton did feel like home, in a way his expensive Seattle condominium and the city he knew best never had.

Lucy, please find me worthy.

LUCY PEERED AT herself in the mirror from between only slightly puffy lids. The cold washcloth had done its job. Chances were good that no one would notice she looked any different than usual, especially once she got bustling in the kitchen over hot burners.

She'd considered not going in. Shea could have filled in for her, or even Samantha in a pinch. But giving herself something to do was a good thing, and anyway, this was her life. Bleakly Lucy thought, *I chose it.*

She still couldn't quite believe she'd thrown away everything she had ever believed she wanted: a gorgeous man who loved her, the possibility of adventure in the wider world, the chance to escape her overabundant family while still being near enough to see them sometimes. Even the impetus she needed to try out her culinary skills for the benefit of more sophisticated diners.

What kind of fool was she?

But in her heart, she knew she couldn't have made a different choice. Adrian's decision to institutionalize his mother without even exploring alternatives made a mockery of all the times they'd talked about the mother he remembered, a woman who had shaped the man he was despite her absence from so much of his life. That man, Lucy had imagined, could be playful, protective, soft-hearted, impulsive. He would be the perfect father. She'd *seen* him in her mind's eye, out on the lawn spinning a little boy in circles, both of them laughing, his smiling mother looking on.

Dumb, idealized dreams. Because, obviously, he wasn't that man.

She blinked fiercely to keep tears from flooding her eyes again. It was three o'clock and she needed to get going if she was to be ready for the dinner crowd.

She had started down the stairs when her doorbell rang. Lucy's step checked and she frowned. That was odd. Who would be stopping by at this time of day? Besides her family, of course, who had the annoying habit of letting themselves in without bothering with any nonsense—as her aunt Beth put it—like ringing the doorbell.

Puzzled, Lucy opened the door.

Like a mirage, Adrian and the hat lady stood on her front porch, Adrian tall and so formidably handsome she was cast back to the first time she saw him.

Her throat closed. She was imagining them. Wasn't she?

He cleared his throat. "I'm glad we caught you at home. I was afraid you'd be at the café."

"I…was about to leave."

Expression wary, he was looking at her entirely too closely. He would notice the puffy eyes.

Well, so what! she thought with defiance. He was the one who'd disappointed her. She wouldn't apologize for loving him, or for grieving for what might have been.

"Um…can we come in?"

The hat lady, whose carriage was very erect, even regal, beamed at Lucy. In a very upper-crust British accent, she said, "Your flower beds are lovely! What a talented young lady you are."

"Why, thank you." Lucy smiled at her. "Please. Do come in. May I offer you a cup of tea?"

"That would be nice, but I wonder…" She glanced at the man at her side, then met Lucy's eyes again, some embarrassment in hers. "I dislike asking for a favor, but…I do believe I need to lie down for a bit. My son suggested I might take advantage of your hospitality."

"Of course you can." Lucy resisted the impulse to hug the frail woman. Because, after all, you weren't supposed to touch Her Majesty without permission. "Let me show you upstairs."

The progress was slow. Adrian, watchful, waited at

the bottom. The hat lady was worn out by her day. Lucy showed her into the guest room.

"May I?" she asked, and, given permission, unpinned the hat. She helped her guest take off her shoes and lie down, then spread an afghan over her. "Shall I close the curtains?"

"No." Her friend, the Queen of England, smiled, her eyes closing. "I like the sunlight on my face."

Lucy tiptoed out, pulling the door almost closed. For a moment she paused there, afraid to go down and face Adrian.

Afraid to find out she was wrong about why he'd turned around and driven his mother back to Middleton. But putting it off wouldn't change anything, would it? Lucy drew a deep breath and made herself start down the stairs.

He waited at the bottom, one hand on the newel post, his eyes never leaving hers from the moment she appeared at the top.

"Thank you," he said, nodding upward.

"I've always loved her. Did you think I wouldn't welcome her?"

His jaw knotted. "I meant, for not questioning our reappearance. I don't think she ever understood that we weren't supposed to turn around and come back to Middleton."

She stood two steps from the bottom, where she could still look down at him. "Why did you come back?"

"Because I realized you were right." His voice was raw. He wasn't a man accustomed to admitting to faults. "I didn't listen to her. I thought about my responsibilities, not her needs."

A wave of dizzying relief washed over Lucy. She had to grab the banister for support. She had been right about him after all. No, wrong, at least the last time she saw him.

"I'm sorry," she whispered. "For everything I said. I should have trusted you."

"No." He reached out, his hand stopping just short of covering hers. His fingers curled into a fist and he withdrew it, as if unsure whether his touch was wanted. "No," he said hoarsely. "I needed to hear every word. I almost didn't, you know. I was pretty angry when I left."

"I know." Oh, she yearned for him to take her in his arms! But she wasn't sure that was what he had in mind at all. *He* would still be going back to Seattle. Would he ask her again to go?

She had already answered that question for herself. Yes, yes, yes! Even though she had discovered, after a lifetime of chafing at the bonds of family and small town, that she *belonged* here. But she belonged with him, too; him, most of all. Perhaps, like Dr. Slater's wife, she could persuade Adrian to retire to Middleton someday.

She had hurt him, though, and he was a proud man. He might never ask again. He might not want her.

"I had to explain over and over where we were going," he said. "But nothing I said sunk in. Mom just kept asking whether we were going home after we rode the ferry."

"And so you decided to bring her."

He grimaced. "And thus we're, uh, imposing on you. Do you need to go to work? I can stay here with Mom, or take her over to your sister's once she wakes up."

"What do you have in mind?" Lucy asked. "I mean, for your mom?"

"Well, that depends." He rubbed the back of his neck, as if to ease tension. "Don't you have to go? I could come back tonight to talk to you, when you get home. Or tomorrow."

"Let me see if I can find someone to fill in for me."

She left him standing there and went to the kitchen, where she made a swift phone call. Then she returned and said, "I'm off the hook until Tuesday. Let's sit down."

He nodded and followed her into the living room, where he hesitated until she sat on one end of the sofa, one foot curled beneath her. He chose the other end, close enough that she could see how rigidly he held himself, the strain on his face, the tight line of his mouth.

"I may buy her a house. Or rent her a room, depending on what you think's best."

Oh. He wanted only to talk about arrangements for his mother.

Lucy nodded, as if considering the options.

"Or perhaps, ah, something like a mother-in-law apartment." Even his voice sounded stifled, with a soft burr. Only his eyes were vividly alive, searching her face. "Depending on you."

Not on what she thought best, but *her.* Hope swelled painfully in her chest.

"What do you mean?" she asked carefully.

"I love you. I didn't just bring my mother back. I brought myself back."

Tears overflowed, and she launched herself at him. "Oh, Adrian! This has been the worst day of my life!"

His arms closed around her with bruising force, and he pressed his cheek against the top of her head. "*God.* I was so afraid—"

When he broke off, she pulled back slightly so that she could see his face. The vulnerability there wrenched her heart.

"I thought…you hadn't really loved me. Believing that was easy. Or maybe I never quite believed you did. After my mother left me—"

"You never felt loved again," she said slowly, shocked despite herself.

"Felt?" His face twisted. "I don't think I was. My father…I doubt he knew how."

"Oh, Adrian." Lucy kissed him slowly, sweetly, tasting her tears and knowing he would as well. "*I* love you."

He made an inarticulate sound that vibrated in his chest then kissed her back, his mouth hungry. Passion was there, but the desperation with which they held each other had another cause entirely.

"Can you stay tonight?" Lucy asked, when she could. "I don't care if your mother's in the guest room…."

"I can stay. If you mean it." Her next kiss apparently reassured him. It was a minute before he could continue. "I can stick around until Monday—"

"Really?" She drew back again. "You've missed so much work."

"I'm quitting," he said flatly.

Shaken, Lucy shook her head. She had to have heard wrong. "What?"

"If you want to stay in Middleton, I'll buy Weatherby's practice if he's really prepared to sell. If you don't—"

She interrupted him. "But…you can't possibly *want* to give up being a partner in a major Seattle law firm so that you can…well, defend Bill Bartovich when he gets in a drunken brawl at the tavern."

He actually grinned at her, so handsome he took her breath away. "I thought Middleton had real crime."

"Of course it does. Sometimes. But…mostly, you'd probably be drawing up wills and refereeing property disputes and—"

"Defending drunken loggers?"

"Yes."

He was still smiling, so much tenderness in eyes she'd once considered chilly, Lucy thought she could die happy right that minute. "What you mean is, I could take care of the legal concerns of my friends and neighbors. Instead of defending corporate scum in court."

"Surely you don't feel that way about all your clients."

Adrian made a quick, impatient gesture. "No. Of course not. But I've had increasing doubts lately. Especially—" he cupped her face "—since I met you. I've been…jealous. I want what you have. Family. People who care."

Her eyes filled with tears again.

With his thumbs, he gently brushed the tears away. "If you want to move to Seattle—or anywhere at all— that's okay, too. I'm still quitting the firm. I want to do something different with my life. We can make provisions for Mom."

She couldn't seem to quit crying, even though now her nose was running, too. "Are you sure? I do want to stay here, but not if you'll be unhappy—"

"Never." He pulled her close and let her weep happily against his shoulder. "I was kind of hoping you'd say that. Middleton seems to have cast its spell on me. I like the idea of raising our kids here."

Lucy wept some more. Eventually, she left him long enough to wash her face and blow her nose. She didn't dare even peek at the mirror. He loved her; he wouldn't care that her face was blotchy and puffy and horribly unattractive.

When she returned to him he kissed her as if he hadn't noticed how she looked at all. Lucy found that amazingly satisfying.

Finally, with her cuddled up to him, he said, "On the ferry I flipped through some real estate booklets. I saw a house for sale here in Middleton. A big old place with a carriage house that's been turned into an apartment."

"Oh!" She sat up. "The Andrews house. I've seen the For Sale sign. It's amazing. But...can you afford it?"

"Sure," he said in surprise. "Or we could stay here. Do you own this house?"

Lucy shook her head. "I rent from my uncle Will. Of course he'd never kick me out."

"Do you mind moving? Right after you started your dream garden?"

"No. Oh, no." Darned if she wasn't near to tears again. "I can start again. And that garden will be my own."

Adrian nodded. "I asked you once before, but I think I need to do it again. Will you marry me, Lucy Peterson?"

"Yes. Yes!"

They kissed, and they held each other, and they murmured confidences. He told her that they'd had to wait nearly forty-five minutes in the ferry line on the other side, and he'd gotten the paperback copy of *The Fellowship of the Ring,* with its yellowed pages, out of the trunk and started reading it to his mother.

"She was too tired to go up top once we did get on the ferry, so she took a turn reading to me during the crossing."

"Was it worth the wait?" Lucy asked.

He was silent for a moment. "Yeah. It was pretty gripping. And sitting there, with my mom reading to me, after all these years…" His voice roughened. "Isn't it funny, when you think you have everything you need, and then you discover you didn't. Here I am with my mother, and you, and someplace to call home."

Her chest hurt, she loved him so much. Lucy nodded. "And I have you, and I've found out I don't want to leave home after all."

She could hardly wait to tell the hat lady that miracles happened every day.

* * * * *

"I'm the illegitimate daughter of notoriously scandalous parents, Mr. Milford. Candidates for my hand are unlikely to be lining up at the gates."

"Don't be so quick to discount your charms, my dear. Or the charm of your substantial dowry. Or even your brothers' influence. There are as many reasons to marry as there are marriages."

Annalise snorted. "Oh, yes. Perhaps I shall marry for dynastic reasons, or perhaps for property or influence. After all, a loveless, practical marriage worked out so well for my mother."

"Well, you've routed me on that one. I can think of no suitable rejoinder." Ned rose to his feet and extended his hand. "And since that is the case, let me be the first to wish you a long and happy spinsterhood."

Her mouth gaped open. And then she laughed.

And he froze.

This was the first time, Ned realized. The first time he'd seen her eyes light up and her mouth curl. The first time he'd witnessed her features melded together in glorious accord to produce exquisite beauty.

Unbelievable what a change came over her face. Unheard of what effect her throaty, rasping laughter had on his body. It pounded a beat upon his ear, quickly taken up by his pulse. It echoed through him, finally residing in his stirring nether regions.

So easily she did it, awakened these sensations within him—without any apparent effort at all. And she had called him potentially dangerous? Clearly the intelligent thing for him to do would be to steer clear, to leave her to the tender ministrations of Lord Peter Blackthorne.

"You were right." She smiled up at him as she took his hand and climbed to her feet. "I do feel better."

Ah, well. When had he ever chosen the intelligent path?

He did not relinquish her hand. He used it to pull her in, close enough that he could feel the warmth of her. "At the risk of repeating Lord Peter's mistake and anticipating too much—may I ask if you'll be my partner in battledore tomorrow?"

Her smiled dimmed. Her breath came a little faster. His own had gone shallow, as if he'd just run a race—and lost. He ran his gaze over the appealing lift of her brow and the curious angle of her chin. His index finger twitched.

"I should like that," she said.

His finger trembled again and he lifted it, traced the pink and tender shell of her ear, the unique sweep of her jaw. Her pulse leaped beneath her skin, triggering his own. Slowly he tilted her chin up, waiting for her to object, to step back, to slap his hand away.

She did none of those eminently sensible things. Which left him free to do the entirely impractical thing.

Baby soft, the skin of her lips. Her whole body trembled when he touched her there.

He leaned in. Her eyes closed, even as she stood straight against him, strung as tight as a bow. He pressed his mouth to hers. It was a soft kiss, sweet and chaste. And yet he was hot and hard and as ready as he'd ever been in his life.

She drew back a little. Sighed. Their breath mingled a moment before she slowly backed away.

"Oh," she breathed. Her dark eyes were full of wonder and something that looked like fear. He took a step toward her, but she only shook her head. His outstretched hand fell to his side as she turned to disappear into the wood. This was the first time, Ned realized. The first time, since he'd come to the house party at Welbourne Manor, that he'd seen her eyes light up.

* * * * *

Follow Ned and Annalise's story in May 2009 in
THE DIAMONDS OF WELBOURNE MANOR
Available May 2009 from Harlequin® Historical

Available in the series romance section,
or in the historical romance section,
wherever books are sold.

**We'll be spotlighting a different series
every month throughout 2009
to celebrate our 60th anniversary.**

Look for Harlequin® Historical in May!

Celebrations begin with
a sumptuous Regency house party!

Join three scandalous sisters in

THE DIAMONDS OF
WELBOURNE MANOR

Glittering, scintillating, sensual fun
by Diane Gaston, Deb Marlowe
and Amanda McCabe.

**60 years of Harlequin,
600 years of romance
in Harlequin Historical!**

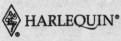

LAURA MARIE ALTOM
The Marine's Babies

Men Made in America

Captain Jace Monroe is everything a Marine
should be—strong, brave and honorable. He's also
an instant father of twin baby girls he never knew
existed! Life gets even more complicated when he
finds himself attracted to Emma Stewart, his new
nanny. But can this sexy, fun-loving bachelor do
the right thing and become a family man?
Emma and the babies are counting on it!

**Available in May
wherever books are sold.**

LOVE, HOME & HAPPINESS

www.eHarlequin.com   HAR75261

REQUEST YOUR FREE BOOKS!

2 FREE NOVELS PLUS 2 FREE GIFTS!

HARLEQUIN®

Super Romance®

Exciting, emotional, unexpected!

YES! Please send me 2 FREE Harlequin® Superromance® novels and my 2 FREE gifts (gifts are worth about $10). After receiving them, if I don't wish to receive any more books, I can return the shipping statement marked "cancel." If I don't cancel, I will receive 6 brand-new novels every month and be billed just $4.69 per book in the U.S. or $5.24 per book in Canada. That's a savings of close to 15% off the cover price! It's quite a bargain! Shipping and handling is just 25¢ per book*. I understand that accepting the 2 free books and gifts places me under no obligation to buy anything. I can always return a shipment and cancel at any time. Even if I never buy another book from Harlequin, the two free books and gifts are mine to keep forever.

135 HDN EEX7   336 HDN EEYK

Name	(PLEASE PRINT)	
Address		Apt. #
City	State/Prov.	Zip/Postal Code

Signature (if under 18, a parent or guardian must sign)

Mail to the Harlequin Reader Service:
IN U.S.A.: P.O. Box 1867, Buffalo, NY 14240-1867
IN CANADA: P.O. Box 609, Fort Erie, Ontario L2A 5X3

Not valid to current subscribers of Harlequin Superromance books.

**Are you a current subscriber of Harlequin Superromance books
and want to receive the larger-print edition?
Call 1-800-873-8635 today!**

* Terms and prices subject to change without notice. Prices do not include applicable taxes. Sales tax applicable in N.Y. Canadian residents will be charged applicable provincial taxes and GST. Offer not valid in Quebec. This offer is limited to one order per household. All orders subject to approval. Credit or debit balances in a customer's account(s) may be offset by any other outstanding balance owed by or to the customer. Please allow 4 to 6 weeks for delivery. Offer available while quantities last.

Your Privacy: Harlequin is committed to protecting your privacy. Our Privacy Policy is available online at www.eHarlequin.com or upon request from the Reader Service. From time to time we make our lists of customers available to reputable third parties who may have a product or service of interest to you. If you would prefer we not share your name and address, please check here. ☐

HSR09